CONTROVERSIES

Poverty
and Homelessness

Other Books in the Current Controversies series

Current CONTROVERSIES

Poverty and Homelessness

Noël Merino, Book Editor

GREENHAVEN PRESS
A part of Gale, Cengage Learning

GALE
CENGAGE Learning

Detroit • New York • San Francisco • New Haven, Conn • Waterville, Maine • London

Christine Nasso, *Publisher*
Elizabeth Des Chenes, *Managing Editor*

© 2009 Greenhaven Press, a part of Gale, Cengage Learning

For more information, contact:
Greenhaven Press
27500 Drake Rd.
Farmington Hills, MI 48331-3535
Or you can visit our Internet site at gale.cengage.com

For product information and technology assistance, contact us at

Gale Customer Support, 1-800-877-4253
For permission to use material from this text or product, submit all requests online at www.cengage.com/permissions

Further permissions questions can be emailed to permissionrequest@cengage.com

Articles in Greenhaven Press anthologies are often edited for length to meet page requirements. In addition, original titles of these works are changed to clearly present the main thesis and to explicitly indicate the author's opinion. Every effort is made to ensure that Greenhaven Press accurately reflects the original intent of the authors. Every effort has been made to trace the owners of copyrighted material.

Cover image copyright Jon Le-Bon, 2009. Used under license from Shutterstock.com.

LIBRARY OF CONGRESS CATALOGING-IN-PUBLICATION DATA

Poverty and homelessness / Noël Merino, book editor.
     p. cm. -- (Current controversies)
Includes bibliographical references and index.
ISBN-13: 978-0-7377-4458-3 (hardcover)
ISBN-13: 978-0-7377-4459-0 (pbk.)
1. Homelessness--United States. 2. Poverty--United States. I. Merino, Noël.
HV4505.P679 2009
362.50973--dc22
                                                                    2009012041

Printed in the United States of America
1 2 3 4 5 6 7 13 12 11 10 09

Contents

Chapter 1: Are Poverty and Homelessness Serious Problems?

Yes: Poverty and Homelessness Are Serious Problems

**No: Poverty and Homelessness Are
Not Serious Problems**

Chapter 2: What Causes Poverty and Homelessness?

Chapter 3: Do Government Welfare Programs Help the Poor?

**Yes: Government Welfare Programs
Help the Poor**

**No: Government Welfare Programs
Do Not Help the Poor**

Chapter 4: What Strategies Would Benefit the Poor and the Homeless?

Foreword

By definition, controversies are "discussions of questions in which opposing opinions clash" (Webster's Twentieth Century Dictionary Unabridged). Few would deny that controversies are a pervasive part of the human condition and exist on virtually every level of human enterprise. Controversies transpire between individuals and among groups, within nations and between nations. Controversies supply the grist necessary for progress by providing challenges and challengers to the status quo. They also create atmospheres where strife and warfare can flourish. A world without controversies would be a peaceful world; but it also would be, by and large, static and prosaic.

The Series' Purpose

The purpose of the Current Controversies series is to explore many of the social, political, and economic controversies dominating the national and international scenes today. Titles selected for inclusion in the series are highly focused and specific. For example, from the larger category of criminal justice, Current Controversies deals with specific topics such as police brutality, gun control, white collar crime, and others. The debates in Current Controversies also are presented in a useful, timeless fashion. Articles and book excerpts included in each title are selected if they contribute valuable, long-range ideas to the overall debate. And wherever possible, current information is enhanced with historical documents and other relevant materials. Thus, while individual titles are current in focus, every effort is made to ensure that they will not become quickly outdated. Books in the Current Controversies series will remain important resources for librarians, teachers, and students for many years.

In addition to keeping the titles focused and specific, great care is taken in the editorial format of each book in the series. Book introductions and chapter prefaces are offered to provide background material for readers. Chapters are organized around several key questions that are answered with diverse opinions representing all points on the political spectrum. Materials in each chapter include opinions in which authors clearly disagree as well as alternative opinions in which authors may agree on a broader issue but disagree on the possible solutions. In this way, the content of each volume in Current Controversies mirrors the mosaic of opinions encountered in society. Readers will quickly realize that there are many viable answers to these complex issues. By questioning each author's conclusions, students and casual readers can begin to develop the critical thinking skills so important to evaluating opinionated material.

Current Controversies is also ideal for controlled research. Each anthology in the series is composed of primary sources taken from a wide gamut of informational categories including periodicals, newspapers, books, U.S. and foreign government documents, and the publications of private and public organizations. Readers will find factual support for reports, debates, and research papers covering all areas of important issues. In addition, an annotated table of contents, an index, a book and periodical bibliography, and a list of organizations to contact are included in each book to expedite further research.

Perhaps more than ever before in history, people are confronted with diverse and contradictory information. During the Persian Gulf War, for example, the public was not only treated to minute-to-minute coverage of the war, it was also inundated with critiques of the coverage and countless analyses of the factors motivating U.S. involvement. Being able to sort through the plethora of opinions accompanying today's major issues, and to draw one's own conclusions, can be a complicated and frustrating struggle. It is the editors' hope that Current Controversies will help readers with this struggle.

Introduction

"Determining the correct measure for poverty is a key issue in determining the extent of the problem of poverty."

Poverty and homelessness are worldwide problems. The extent of poverty and homelessness, their causes, and their best solutions are subject to much debate. Just defining poverty, an essential step for measuring the extent of it, has prompted widely divergent views. Broadly speaking, poverty is the state of having a deficiency of basic necessities such as food, water, health care, clothing, and shelter. For many people suffering from poverty, paying rent or a mortgage becomes impossible, resulting in homelessness. Determining what level of deficiency constitutes a state of poverty is a task that has plagued experts worldwide and sparked significant controversy.

The World Bank defines poverty as living on less than $1.25 per day (at 2005 prices, adjusted to account for the differences in purchasing power across countries). According to this measure, there is no poverty in the United States, Canada, Australia, New Zealand, and the countries of Western Europe. According to the World Bank, as of August 2008, 1.4 billion people in the developing world were living on less than $1.25 a day and thus qualified as living in poverty.[1] This number amounts to over 20 percent of the world's population, and some say it sets the bar for poverty too low.

Columbia University economics professor Sanjay Reddy claims that "the [World] Bank's chosen international poverty line is far too low to cover the cost of purchasing basic necessities."[2] Reddy notes that no person in the United States could live on an amount close to $1.25 per day. Since purchasing power in the United States forms the basis of the measure in other countries, Reddy argues that if the measure is flawed in the United States, it is probably flawed everywhere. If the World Bank's definition fails to measure poverty in the United States, then it must vastly underestimate the amount of poverty around the world.

In the United States, the Census Bureau sets the official poverty line. The figure used to compute a person's poverty status includes any earnings, Social Security payments, child support, or other assistance. Then, using the size of the family and the ages of the family members, the Census Bureau determines which poverty threshold applies; for example, in 2007 a family of four that included two children would be considered in poverty if their total income was less than $21,027 for the year. According to this poverty measure, 12.5 percent of the U.S. population lived in poverty in 2007.

Many commentators believe that the poverty line set by the U.S. Census Bureau ends up overstating the number of poor in the United States. Commentator Bruce Bartlett believes the U.S. Census Bureau measure is far too generous, arguing that many who qualify as poor under the Census Bureau's guidelines own their own homes or own major appliances; he argues that the measure is too simplistic and ends up classifying people who live well as poor. Rea Hederman of the Heritage Foundation argues that the measurement is flawed because it fails to take into account government transfer programs that work to alleviate poverty, thus underestimating many families' actual wealth

On the other side, however, are those who argue that the official U.S. poverty measure *understates* the number of poor. The National Center for Children in Poverty (NCCP) asserts that the measure is based on an outdated calculation that was established over forty years ago when food constituted about one-third of the family income, thus setting the poverty level by multiplying average food costs by a factor of three. Researchers at the NCCP argue that since "food now comprises far less than a third of an average family's expenses, while the costs of housing, child care, health care, and transportation have grown disproportionately," the poverty level set by the Census Bureau does not accurately portray the true cost of supporting a family.[3] Other critics argue that by failing to take into account geographical differences in costs, the poverty line is out of touch with the real costs of living, at least in some states. The California Budget Project points out that the poverty line in 2006 for a family of four with two children was $20,444, but the minimum budget for a family of four in California with one working parent was realistically $50,383.

Determining the correct measure for poverty is a key issue in determining the extent of the problem of poverty. An accurate assessment of the extent of poverty can significantly aid the exploration of the causes of poverty and effective solutions. By presenting different views on the extent of poverty and homelessness in the United States and proposed solutions for combating these two problems, *Current Controversies: Poverty and Homelessness* sheds light on this important social issue.

Notes

1. World Bank, Understanding Poverty, accessed January 5, 2009. http://web.worldbank.org/WBSITE/EXTERNAL/ TOPICS/EXTPOVERTY/EXTPA/0,,contentMDK:20153855~ menuPK:435040~pagePK:148956~piPK:216618~theSitePK:4303 67,00.html.

2. Sanjay Reddy, "The World Bank's New Poverty Estimates— Digging Deeper into a Hole," International Development Economics Associates (IDEAs), August 28, 2008. www.networkideas.org. www.networkideas.org/themes/world/aug2008/ we28_World_Bank.htm.

3. Nancy K. Cauthen and Sarah Fass, "Measuring Income and Poverty in the United States," National Center for Children in Poverty (NCCP), April 2007. http://nccp.org/publications/ pub_707.html.

CHAPTER 1

Are Poverty and Homelessness Serious Problems?

Poverty: An Overview

Bernadette D. Proctor

Bernadette D. Proctor works in the Housing and Household Economic Statistics Division of the U.S. Census Bureau.

The official poverty rate in 2007 was 12.5 percent, not statistically different from 2006.

In 2007, 37.3 million people were in poverty, up from 36.5 million in 2006.

Poverty rates in 2007 were statistically unchanged for non-Hispanic Whites (8.2 percent), Blacks (24.5 percent), and Asians (10.2 percent) from 2006. The poverty rate increased for Hispanics (21.5 percent in 2007, up from 20.6 percent in 2006).

The poverty rate in 2007 was lower than in 1959, the first year for which poverty estimates are available, while statistically higher than the most recent trough in 2000 (11.3 percent).

The poverty rate increased for children under 18 years old (18.0 percent in 2007, up from 17.4 percent in 2006), while it remained statistically unchanged for people 18 to 64 years old (10.9 percent) and people 65 and over (9.7 percent).

The Impact of Race and Age

At 8.2 percent, the 2007 poverty rate for non-Hispanic Whites was lower than the rate for Blacks and Asians—24.5 percent and 10.2 percent, respectively. For all three of these groups, the number and the percentage in poverty were statistically unchanged between 2006 and 2007. In 2007, non-Hispanic Whites accounted for 43.0 percent of people in poverty while

Carmen DeNavas-Walt, Bernadette D. Proctor, and Jessica C. Smith, U.S. Census Bureau, Current Population Reports, P60-235, *Income, Poverty, and Health Insurance Coverage in the United States: 2007*. Washington, DC: U.S. Government Printing Office, August 2008. Reproduced by permission.

representing 65.8 percent of the total population. Among Hispanics, 21.5 percent (9.9 million) were in poverty in 2007, higher than the 20.6 percent (9.2 million) in 2006.

In 2007, both the poverty rate and the number in poverty increased for children under 18 years old.

Both the poverty rate and the number in poverty for people aged 18 to 64 were not statistically different in 2007 than in 2006, at 10.9 percent and 20.4 million in 2007. The poverty rate for people 65 and older remained statistically unchanged at 9.7 percent, while the number in poverty increased to 3.6 million in 2007 from 3.4 million in 2006.

In 2007, both the poverty rate and the number in poverty increased for children under 18 years old (18.0 percent and 13.3 million in 2007, up from 17.4 percent and 12.8 million in 2006). The poverty rate for children was higher than the rates for people 18 to 64 years old and those 65 and older. Children represented 35.7 percent of the people in poverty and 24.8 percent of the total population.

Estimates for related children under 18 include children related to the householder (or the reference person of an unrelated subfamily) who are not themselves a householder or spouse of the householder (or the family reference person). Both the poverty rate and the number in poverty increased for related children under 18 living in families (17.6 percent and 12.8 million in 2007, up from 16.9 percent and 12.3 million in 2006). For related children under 18 living in families with a female householder with no husband present, 43.0 percent were in poverty, compared with 8.5 percent for children in married-couple families.

The poverty rate for related children under 6 was 20.8 percent in 2007, statistically unchanged from 2006, while the number in poverty increased to 5.1 million in 2007, up from 4.8 million in 2006. Of related children under 6 with female householders with no husband present, 54.0 percent were in poverty, over five times the rate of their counter-parts in married-couple families (9.5 percent).

National Origin and Current Location

Of all people, 87.5 percent were native born and 12.5 percent were foreign born. The poverty rate and the number in poverty for the native-born population, 11.9 percent and 31.1 million in 2007, were not statistically different from any of the three previous years—2004 to 2006. The poverty rate and the number in poverty for the foreign-born population increased to 16.5 percent and 6.2 million in 2007 from 15.2 percent and 5.7 million in 2006.

Of the foreign-born population, 40.4 percent were naturalized citizens; the remaining were noncitizens. The poverty rate in 2007 was 9.5 percent for foreign-born naturalized citizens, statistically unchanged from 2006. The poverty rate in 2007 was 21.3 percent for those who were not U.S. citizens, up from 19.0 percent in 2006.

The number in poverty in the South increased to 15.5 million in 2007, up from 14.9 million in 2006, while the poverty rate remained statistically unchanged at 14.2 percent in 2007. In 2007, the poverty rate for the Northeast (11.4 percent), the Midwest (11.1 percent), and the West (12.0 percent) were all statistically unchanged from 2006.

Inside metropolitan statistical areas, the poverty rate and the number of people in poverty were 11.9 percent and 29.9 million in 2007, both statistically unchanged from 2006. Of all people in metropolitan statistical areas in 2007, 38.5 percent lived in principal cities, and 53.4 percent of people in poverty in those metropolitan areas lived in principal cities.

The number in poverty increased for people in principal cities to 16.0 million in 2007, from 15.3 million in 2006, while their poverty rate remained statistically unchanged at 16.5 percent in 2007. The poverty rate and the number in poverty for those not in principal cities were 9.0 percent and 13.9 million in 2007, statistically unchanged from 2006.

The poverty rate and the number in poverty showed no statistical change between 2006 and 2007 for the different types of families.

Among those living outside metropolitan statistical areas, the poverty rate and the number in poverty were 15.4 percent and 7.4 million in 2007, statistically unchanged from 2006.

Work Experience and Family Structure

People 16 and older who worked some or all of 2007 had a lower poverty rate than those who did not work at any time, 5.7 percent compared with 21.5 percent. The poverty rate among full-time, year-round workers (2.5 percent) was lower than the rate for those who worked part-time or part-year (12.7 percent) in 2007. In addition, among people 16 and older, those who did not work in 2007 represented 43.5 percent of people in poverty and 25.2 percent of all people.

In 2007, the poverty rate and the number of families in poverty were 9.8 percent and 7.6 million, both statistically unchanged from 2006.

Furthermore, the poverty rate and the number in poverty showed no statistical change between 2006 and 2007 for the different types of families. In 2007, the poverty rates for married-couple families (4.9 percent and 2.8 million), female-householder-with-no-husband-present families (28.3 percent and 4.1 million), and male-householder-with-no-wife-present families (13.6 percent and 696,000) were all statistically unchanged from 2006.

The Depth of Poverty

Categorizing people as "in poverty" or "not in poverty" is one way to describe their economic situation. The income-to-poverty ratio and the income deficit (surplus) describe other aspects of economic well-being. Where the poverty rate provides a measure of the proportion of people with a family income that is below the established poverty thresholds, the income-to-poverty ratio provides a measure to gauge the depth of poverty and to calculate the size of the population who may be eligible for government-sponsored assistance programs, such as Temporary Assistance for Needy Families (TANF), Medicare, food stamps, and the Low-Income Home Energy Assistance Program (LIHEAP). The income-to-poverty ratio is reported as a percentage that compares a family's or an unrelated individual's (people who do not live with relatives) income with their poverty threshold. For example, a family or individual with an income-to-poverty ratio of 110 percent has income that is 10 percent above their poverty threshold.

In 2007, 5.2 percent, or 15.6 million people, had an income below one-half of their poverty threshold.

The income deficit (surplus) tells how many dollars a family's or an unrelated individual's income is below (above) their poverty threshold. These measures illustrate how the low-income population varies in relation to the poverty thresholds. . . .

In 2007, 5.2 percent, or 15.6 million people, had an income below one-half of their poverty threshold. This group represented 41.8 percent of the poverty population in 2007. The percentage and number of people with income below 125 percent of their threshold was 17.0 percent and 50.9 million. For children under 18 years old, 7.8 percent (5.8 million) were below 50 percent of their poverty thresholds and 23.8 percent (17.6 million) were below 125 percent of their thresholds.

The demographic makeup of the population differs at varying degrees of poverty. In 2007 among all people, 5.2 percent were below 50 percent of their threshold, 7.3 percent were above 50 percent and below 100 percent of their threshold, and 4.6 percent were between 100 percent and 125 percent of their threshold. The 65-and-older population was more highly concentrated between 100 percent and 125 percent of their poverty thresholds (6.4 percent) than below 50 percent of their thresholds (2.5 percent). Among people 65 and older, 9.7 percent were below 100 percent of poverty and 16.1 percent were below 125 percent of poverty—a 66.0 percent difference. The distribution was different for all people— 12.5 percent were below 100 percent of poverty and 17.0 percent were below 125 percent of poverty, a 36.0 percent difference.

For unrelated individuals in poverty, the average income deficit was $5,609 in 2007.

Income Deficit for Those in Poverty

The income deficit for families in poverty (the difference in dollars between a family's income and its poverty threshold) averaged $8,523 in 2007, higher in real terms than the 2006 figure ($8,032). The average income deficit was larger for families with a female householder with no husband present ($9,059) than for married-couple families ($7,937) and families with a male householder with no wife present ($7,780).

The income deficit per capita for families with a female householder with no husband present, ($2,741) was higher than for married-couple families ($2,073). The income deficit per capita is computed by dividing the average deficit by the average number of people in that type of family. Because families with a female householder with no husband present were smaller, on average, than married-couple families, the larger per capita deficit for female-householder families with no husband present reflects their smaller family size as well as their lower income. For unrelated individuals in poverty, the average income deficit was $5,609 in 2007. The $5,377 deficit for women was lower than the $5,920 deficit for men.

U.S. Poverty Rates Are the Highest in the Developed World

Paul Harris

Paul Harris is a British journalist for the London newspaper
The Observer.

The flickering television in Candy Lumpkins's trailer blared out *The Bold and the Beautiful*. It was a fantasy daytime soap vision of American life with little relevance to the reality of this impoverished corner of Kentucky. The Lumpkinses live at the definition of the back of beyond, in a hollow at the top of a valley at the end of a long and muddy dirt road. It is strewn with litter. Packs of stray dogs prowl around, barking at strangers. There is no telephone and since their pump broke two weeks ago Candy has collected water from nearby springs. Oblivious to it all, her five-year-old daughter Amy runs barefoot on a wooden porch frozen by a midwinter chill.

A Shocking Amount of Poverty

It is a vision of deep and abiding poverty. Yet the Lumpkins are not alone in their plight. They are just the negative side of the American equation. America does have vast, wealthy suburbs, huge shopping malls and a busy middle class, but it also has vast numbers of poor, struggling to make it in a low-wage economy with minimal government help.

A shocking 37 million Americans live in poverty. That is 12.7 per cent of the population—the highest percentage in the developed world. They are found from the hills of Kentucky to Detroit's streets, from the Deep South of Louisiana to the heartland of Oklahoma. Each year since 2001 their number has grown.

Paul Harris, "37 Million Poor Hidden in the Land of Plenty," *Observer*, February 19, 2006, p. 32. Reproduced by permission of Guardian News Service, LTD.

Under President George W Bush an extra 5.4 million have slipped below the poverty line. Yet they are not a story of the unemployed or the destitute. Most have jobs. Many have two. Amos Lumpkins has work and his children go to school. But the economy, stripped of worker benefits like healthcare, is having trouble providing good wages.

Even families with two working parents are often one slice of bad luck—a medical bill or factory closure—away from disaster. The minimum wage of $5.15 (£2.95) an hour has not risen since 1997 and, adjusted for inflation, is at its lowest since 1956. The gap between the haves and the have-nots looms wider than ever. Faced with rising poverty rates, Bush's trillion-dollar federal budget recently raised massive amounts of defence spending for the war in Iraq and slashed billions from welfare programmes.

No Focus on Poverty

For a brief moment [in 2005] in New Orleans, Hurricane Katrina brought America's poor into the spotlight. Poverty seemed on the government's agenda. That spotlight has now been turned off. 'I had hoped Katrina would have changed things more. It hasn't,' says Cynthia Duncan, a sociology professor at the University of New Hampshire.

Wal-Mart embodies the new American job market: low wages, few benefits.

Oklahoma is in America's heartland. Tulsa looks like picture-book Middle America. Yet there is hunger here. When it comes to the most malnourished poor in America, Oklahoma is ahead of any other state. It should be impossible to go hungry here. But it is not. Just ask those gathered at a food handout. They are a cross section of society: black, white, young couples, pensioners and the middle-aged. A few are out of work or retired, everyone else has jobs.

They are people like Freda Lee, 33, who has two jobs, as a marketer and a cashier. She has come to the nondescript Loaves and Fishes building—flanked ironically by a Burger King and a McDonald's—to collect food for herself and three sons. 'America is meant to be free. What's free?' she laughs. 'All we can do is pay off the basics.'

Or they are people like Tammy Reinbold, 37. She works part-time and her husband works full-time. They have two children yet rely on the food handouts. 'The church is all we have to fall back on,' she says. She is right. When government help is being cut and wages are insufficient, churches often fill the gap. The needy gather to receive food boxes. They listen to a preacher for half an hour on the literal truth of the Bible. Then he asks them if they want to be born again. Three women put up their hands.

Relying on Charities

But why are some Tulsans hungry? Many believe it is the changing face of the US economy. Tulsa has been devastated by job losses. Big-name firms like WorldCom, Williams Energy and CitGo have closed or moved, costing the city about 24,000 jobs. Now Wal-Mart embodies the new American job market: low wages, few benefits.

Well-paid work only goes to the university-educated. Many others who just complete high school face a bleak future. In Texas more than a third of students entering public high schools now drop out. These people are entering the fragile world of the working poor, where each day is a mere step away from tragedy. Some of those tragedies in Tulsa end up in the care of Steve Whitaker, a pastor who runs a homeless mission in the shadow of a freeway overpass.

Each day the homeless and the drug addicted gather here, looking for a bed for the night. Some also want a fresh chance. They are men like Mark Schloss whose disaster was being left by his first wife. The former Wal-Mart manager entered a world of drug addiction and alcoholism until he wound up with Whitaker. Now he is back on track, sporting a silver ring that says Faith, Hope, Love. 'Without this place I would be in prison or dead,' he says. But Whitaker equates saving lives with saving souls. Those entering the mission's rehabilitation programme are drilled in Bible studies and Christianity. At 6ft 5in and with a black belt in karate, Whitaker's Christianity is muscular both literally and figuratively. 'People need God in their lives,' he says.

These are mean streets. Tulsa is a city divided like the country. Inside a building run by Whitaker's staff in northern Tulsa a group of 'latch-key kids' are taking Bible classes after school while they wait for parents to pick them up. One of them is Taylor Finley, aged nine. Wearing a T-shirt with an American flag on the front, she dreams of travel. 'I want to have fun in a new place, a new country,' she says. Taylor wants to see the world outside Oklahoma. But at the moment she cannot even see her own neighbourhood. The centre in which she waits for mom was built without windows on its ground floor. It was the only way to keep out bullets from the gangs outside.

Two Americas

During the 2004 [presidential] election the only politician to address poverty directly was John Edwards, whose campaign theme was 'Two Americas'. He was derided by Republicans for doing down the country and—after John Kerry picked him as his Democratic running mate—the rhetoric softened in the heat of the campaign.

But, in fact, Edwards was right. While 45.8 million Americans lack any health insurance, the top 20 per cent of earners take over half the national income. At the same time the bottom 20 per cent took home just 3.4 per cent. Whitaker put the figures into simple English. 'The poor have got poorer and the rich have got richer,' he said.

Dealing with poverty is not a viable political issue in America. It jars with a cultural sense that the poor bring things upon themselves and that every American is born with the same chances in life. It also runs counter to the strong anti-government current in modern American politics. Yet the problem will not disappear. 'There is a real sense of impending crisis, but political leaders have little motivation to address this growing divide,' Cynthia Duncan says.

There is little doubt which side of America's divide the hills of east Kentucky fall on. Driving through the wooded Appalachian valleys is a lesson in poverty. The mountains have never been rich. Times now are as tough as they have ever been. Trailer homes are the norm. Every so often a lofty mansion looms into view, a sign of prosperity linked to the coal mines or the logging firms that are the only industries in the region. Everyone else lives on the margins, grabbing work where they can. The biggest cash crop is illicitly grown marijuana.

A Global Poverty Organization in Kentucky

Save The Children works here. Though the charity is usually associated with earthquakes in Pakistan or famine in Africa, it runs an extensive programme in east Kentucky. It includes a novel scheme enlisting teams of 'foster grandparents' to tackle the shocking child illiteracy rates and thus eventually hit poverty itself.

The problem is acute. At Jone's Fork school, a team of indomitable grannies arrive each day to read with the children. The scheme has two benefits: it helps the children struggle out of poverty and pays the pensioners a small wage. 'This has been a lifesaver for me and I feel as if the children would just fall through the cracks without us,' says Erma Owens. It has offered dramatic help to some. One group of children are doing so well in the scheme that their teacher, Loretta Shepherd, has postponed retirement in order to stand by them. 'It renewed me to have these kids,' she said.

In America, ... those in poverty are often blamed for their own situation. Experience on the ground does little to bear that out.

Certainly Renae Sturgill sees the changes in her children. She too lives in deep poverty. Though she attends college and her husband has a job, the Sturgill trailer sits amid a clutter of abandoned cars. Money is scarce. But now her kids are in the reading scheme and she has seen how they have changed. Especially eight-year-old Zach. He's hard to control at times, but he has come to love school. 'Zach likes reading now. I know it's going to be real important for him,' Renae says. Zach is shy and won't speak much about his achievements. But Genny Waddell, who co-ordinates family welfare at Jone's Fork, is immensely proud. 'Now Zach reads because he wants to. He really fought to get where he is,' she says.

Ignoring the Poor

In America, to be poor is a stigma. In a country which celebrates individuality and the goal of giving everyone an equal opportunity to make it big, those in poverty are often blamed for their own situation. Experience on the ground does little to bear that out. When people are working two jobs at a time and still failing to earn enough to feed their families, it seems impossible to call them lazy or selfish. There seems to be a failure in the system, not the poor themselves.

It is an impression backed up by many of those mired in poverty in Oklahoma and Kentucky. Few asked for handouts. Many asked for decent wages. 'It is unfair. I am working all the time and so what have I done wrong?' says Freda Lee. But the economy does not seem to be allowing people to make a decent living. It condemns the poor to stay put, fighting against seemingly impossible odds or to pull up sticks and try somewhere else.

In Tulsa, Tammy Reinbold and her family are moving to Texas as soon as they save the money for enough petrol. It could take several months. 'I've been in Tulsa 12 years and I just gotta try somewhere else,' she says.

In a country that prides itself on a culture of rugged individualism, hard work and self-sufficiency, it is no surprise that poverty and the poor do not have a central place in America's cultural psyche.

But in art, films and books American poverty has sometimes been portrayed with searing honesty. John Steinbeck's novel *The Grapes of Wrath*, which was made into a John Ford[-directed] movie, is the most famous example. It was an unflinching account of the travails of a poor Oklahoma family forced to flee the Dust Bowl during the 1930s Depression. Its portrait of Tom Joad and his family's life on the road as they sought work was a nod to wider issues of social justice in America.

Another ground-breaking work of that time was James Agee's *Let Us Now Praise Famous Men*, a non-fiction book about time spent among poor white farmers in the Deep South. It practically disappeared upon its first publication in 1940 but in the Sixties was hailed as a masterpiece. In mainstream American culture, poverty often lurks in the background. Or it is portrayed—as in Sergio Leone's crime epic *Once Upon A Time In America*—as the basis for a tale of rags to riches.

There are 82,000 homeless people in Los Angeles alone.

One notable, yet often overlooked, exception was the great success of the sitcom *Roseanne*. The show depicted the realities of working-class Middle American life with a grit and humour that is a world away from the usual sitcom settings in a sunlit suburbia, most often in New York or California. The biggest sitcoms of the past decade—*Friends, Frasier* or *Will and Grace*—all deal with aspirational middle-class foibles that have little relevance to America's millions of working poor.

An America Divided

- There are 37 million Americans living below the poverty line. That figure has increased by five million since President George W. Bush came to power.

- The United States has 269 billionaires, the highest number in the world.

- Almost a quarter of all black Americans live below the poverty line; 22 per cent of Hispanics fall below it. But for whites the figure is just 8.6 per cent.

- There are 46 million Americans without health insurance.

- There are 82,000 homeless people in Los Angeles alone.

- In 2004 the poorest community in America was Pine Ridge Indian reservation. Unemployment is over 80 per cent, 69 per cent of people live in poverty and male life expectancy is 57 years. In the Western hemisphere only Haiti has a lower number.

- The richest town in America is Rancho Santa Fe in California. Average incomes are more than $100,000 a year; the average house price is $1.7m [million].

Severe Poverty Is on the Rise in America

Tony Pugh

Tony Pugh is a reporter who covers consumer economics for Mc-Clatchy Newspapers.

The percentage of poor Americans who are living in severe poverty has reached a 32-year high, millions of working Americans are falling closer to the poverty line and the gulf between the nation's "haves" and "have-nots" continues to widen.

A McClatchy Newspapers analysis of 2005 census figures, the latest available [as of February 2007], found that nearly 16 million Americans are living in deep or severe poverty. A family of four with two children and an annual income of less than $9,903—half the federal poverty line—was considered severely poor in 2005. So were individuals who made less than $5,080 a year.

Severe Poverty on the Rise

The McClatchy analysis found that the number of severely poor Americans grew by 26 percent from 2000 to 2005. That's 56 percent faster than the overall number of poor people grew in the same period. McClatchy's review also found statistically significant increases in the percentage of the population in severe poverty in 65 of 215 large U.S. counties, and similar increases in 28 states. The review also suggested that the rise in severely poor people isn't confined to large urban counties but extends to suburban and rural areas.

The plight of the severely poor is a distressing sidebar to an unusual economic expansion. Worker productivity has increased dramatically since the brief recession of 2001, but wages and job growth have lagged. At the same time, the share of national income going to corporate profits has dwarfed the amount going to wages and salaries. That helps explain why the median household income of working-age families, adjusted for inflation, has fallen for five straight years.

These and other factors have helped push 43 percent of the nation's 37 million poor people into deep poverty, the highest rate since at least 1975.

The share of poor Americans in deep poverty has climbed slowly but steadily over the past three decades. But since 2000, the number of severely poor has grown "more than any other segment of the population," according to a recent study in the *American Journal of Preventive Medicine*.

About one in three severely poor people are under age 17, and nearly two out of three are female.

"That was the exact opposite of what we anticipated when we began," said Dr. Steven Woolf of Virginia Commonwealth University, who co-authored the study. "We're not seeing as much moderate poverty as a proportion of the population. What we're seeing is a dramatic growth of severe poverty."

The growth spurt, which leveled off in 2005, in part reflects how hard it is for low-skilled workers to earn their way out of poverty in an unstable job market that favors skilled and educated workers. It also suggests that social programs aren't as effective as they once were at catching those who fall into economic despair.

About one in three severely poor people are under age 17, and nearly two out of three are female. Female-headed families with children account for a large share of the severely poor.

According to census data, nearly two of three people in severe poverty are white (10.3 million) and 6.9 million are non-

Hispanic whites. Severely poor blacks (4.3 million) are more than three times as likely as non-Hispanic whites to be in deep poverty, while extremely poor Hispanics of any race (3.7 million) are more than twice as likely.

Washington, D.C., the nation's capital, has a higher concentration of severely poor people—10.8 percent in 2005—than any of the 50 states, topping even hurricane-ravaged Mississippi and Louisiana, with 9.3 percent and 8.3 percent, respectively. Nearly six of 10 poor District residents are in extreme poverty.

Not Getting Help

A few miles from the Capitol Building, 60-year-old John Treece pondered his life in deep poverty as he left a local food pantry with two bags of free groceries.

Plagued by arthritis, back problems and myriad ailments from years of manual labor, Treece has been unable to work full time for 15 years. He has tried unsuccessfully to get benefits from the Social Security Administration, which he said disputes his injuries and work history.

In 2006, an extremely poor individual earned less than $5,244 a year, according to federal poverty guidelines. Treece said he earned about that much in 2006 doing odd jobs.

Wearing shoes with holes, a tattered plaid jacket and a battered baseball cap, Treece lives hand to mouth in a $450-a-month room in a nondescript boarding house in a high-crime neighborhood. Thanks to food stamps, the food pantry and help from relatives, Treece said he never goes hungry. But toothpaste, soap, toilet paper and other items that require cash are tougher to come by.

Treece remains positive and humble despite his circumstances.

"I don't ask for nothing," he said. "I just thank the Lord for this day and ask that tomorrow be just as blessed."

Like Treece, many who did physical labor during their peak earning years have watched their job prospects dim as their bodies gave out.

Severe poverty is worst near the Mexican border and in some areas of the South, where 6.5 million severely poor residents are struggling to find work as manufacturing jobs in the textile, apparel and furniture-making industries disappear. The Midwestern Rust Belt and areas of the Northeast also have been hard-hit as economic restructuring and foreign competition have forced numerous plant closings.

At the same time, low-skilled immigrants with impoverished family members are increasingly drawn to the South and Midwest to work in the meatpacking, food processing and agricultural industries.

"What appears to be taking place is that, over the long term, you have a significant permanent underclass that is not being impacted by anti-poverty policies," said Michael Tanner, the director of Health and Welfare Studies at the Cato Institute, a libertarian think tank.

Arloc Sherman, a senior researcher at the Center on Budget and Policy Priorities, a liberal think tank, disagreed. "It doesn't look like a growing permanent underclass," said Sherman, whose organization has chronicled the growth of deep poverty. "What you see in the data are more and more single moms with children who lose their jobs and who aren't being caught by a safety net anymore."

About 1.1 million such families account for roughly 2.1 million deeply poor children, Sherman said.

The "Sinkhole Effect"

After fleeing an abusive marriage in 2002, 42-year-old Marjorie Sant moved with her three children from Arkansas to a seedy boarding house in Raleigh, N.C., where the four shared one bedroom. For most of 2005, they lived off food stamps and the $300 a month in Social Security Disability Income for her son with attention deficit hyperactivity disorder. Teachers offered clothes to Sant's children. Saturdays meant lunch at the Salvation Army.

"To depend on other people to feed and clothe your kids is horrible," Sant said. "I found myself in a hole and didn't know how to get out."

In the summer of 2005, social workers warned that she'd lose her children if her home situation didn't change. Sant then brought her two youngest children to a temporary housing program at the Raleigh Rescue Mission while her oldest son moved to California to live with an adult daughter from a previous marriage.

So for 10 months, Sant learned basic office skills. She now lives in a rented house, works two jobs and earns about $20,400 a year.

Sant is proud of where she is, but she knows that "if something went wrong, I could well be back to where I was."

As more poor Americans sink into severe poverty, more individuals and families living within $8,000 above or below the poverty line also have seen their incomes decline. Steven Woolf of Virginia Commonwealth University attributes this to what he calls a "sinkhole effect" on income.

"Just as a sinkhole causes everything above it to collapse downward, families and individuals in the middle and upper classes appear to be migrating to lower-income tiers that bring them closer to the poverty threshold," Woolf wrote in the study.

Before Hurricane Katrina, Rene Winn of Biloxi, [Mississippi,] earned $28,000 a year as an administrator for the Boys & Girls Club. But for 11 months in 2006, she couldn't find steady work and wouldn't take a fast-food job. As her opportunities dwindled, Winn's frustration grew.

After relocating to New Jersey for 10 months after the storm, Winn returned to Biloxi in September [2006] because of medical and emotional problems with her son. She and her two youngest children moved into her sister's home along with her mother, who has Alzheimer's. With her sister, brother-in-law and their two children, eight people now share a three-bedroom home.

Winn said she recently took a job as a technician at the state health department. The hourly job pays $16,120 a year. That's enough to bring her out of severe poverty and just $122 shy of the $16,242 needed for a single mother with two children to escape poverty altogether under current federal guidelines.

Winn eventually wants to transfer to a higher-paying job, but she's thankful for her current position.

America has had the highest or near-highest poverty rates for children, individual adults and families among 31 developed countries.

"I'm very independent and used to taking care of my own, so I don't like the fact that I have to depend on the state. I want to be able to do it myself."

Many Americans Experience Poverty Sometime

The Census Bureau's Survey of Income and Program Participation shows that, in a given month, only 10 percent of severely poor Americans received Temporary Assistance for Needy Families in 2003—the latest year available—and that only 36 percent received food stamps.

Many could have exhausted their eligibility for welfare or decided that the new program requirements were too onerous. But the low participation rates are troubling because the worst by-products of poverty, such as higher crime and violence rates and poor health, nutrition and educational outcomes, are worse for those in deep poverty.

Over the past two decades, America has had the highest or near-highest poverty rates for children, individual adults and families among 31 developed countries, according to the Luxembourg Income Study, a 23-year project that compares poverty and income data from 31 industrial nations.

With the exception of Mexico and Russia, the U.S. devotes the smallest portion of its gross domestic product to federal anti-poverty programs, and those programs are among the least effective at reducing poverty, the study found. Again, only Russia and Mexico do worse jobs.

One in three Americans will experience a full year of extreme poverty at some point in his or her adult life, according to long-term research by Mark Rank, a professor of social welfare at Washington University in St. Louis.

An estimated 58 percent of Americans between the ages of 20 and 75 will spend at least a year in poverty, Rank said. Two of three will use a public-assistance program between ages 20 and 65, and 40 percent will do so for five years or more.

Alternative poverty measures ... typically inflate or deflate official poverty statistics [but] ... show the same kind of long-term trends as the official poverty data.

These estimates don't include illegal immigrants. Rank said if illegal immigrants were factored in, the numbers would be worse.

"It would appear that for most Americans the question is no longer if, but rather when, they will experience poverty. In short, poverty has become a routine and unfortunate part of the American life course," Rank wrote in a recent study.

Poverty Measures Exclude Many Poor

Most researchers and economists say federal poverty estimates are a poor tool to gauge the complexity of poverty. The numbers don't factor in assistance from government anti-poverty programs, such as food stamps, housing subsidies and the Earned Income Tax Credit, all of which increase incomes and help pull people out of poverty.

But federal poverty measures also exclude work-related expenses and necessities such as day care, transportation, housing and health-care costs, which eat up large portions of disposable income, particularly for low-income families.

Alternative poverty measures that account for these shortcomings typically inflate or deflate official poverty statistics. But many of those alternative measures show the same kind of long-term trends as the official poverty data.

Robert Rector, a senior researcher with the Heritage Foundation, a conservative think tank, questioned the growth of severe poverty, saying that census data become less accurate further down the income ladder. He said many poor people, particularly single mothers with boyfriends, underreport their income by not including cash gifts and loans. Rector said he has seen no data that suggest increasing deprivation among the very poor.

Homelessness in America Is a Growing Problem

Jim Romeo

Jim Romeo is a writer based in Chesapeake, Virginia.

Tony, 48 years old, spent 15 years as a Navy yeoman and now receives $361 a month in disability payments from the Veterans Administration. He panhandles for extra cash around Norfolk, Virginia, and has been homeless for three years.

Tony is far from alone. According to a survey announced in early October [2005] by *USA Today*, more than 727,000 individuals were homeless in 460 communities [in spring 2005].

However, about 3.5 million Americans are likely to experience homelessness in any given year—not counting the many thousands set adrift after Hurricanes Katrina and Rita decimated the Gulf Coast. Billions in emergency funds are being spent to help the hurricane victims, and billions more are spent each year to control the nation's perennial homelessness problem.

The [George W.] Bush administration's proposed budget for fiscal 2006 includes $528.5 billion for homelessness programs administered through HUD [Department of Housing and Urban Development] and a $1 billion increase for Section 8 [low-income] housing. It also includes $1.4 billion for Homeless Assistance Grants, $200 million more than in 2005. Altogether, the administration has requested $4 billion in 2006 for federal housing and social programs for the homeless—an increase of 8.5 percent.

Homelessness was growing even before Hurricane Katrina made it worse. In 1997, research conducted in 11 communities and four states by the National Coalition for the Homeless found that shelter capacity had more than doubled in nine communities and three states in the previous decade.

A New Strategy

According to Dan Straughan, executive director of the Homeless Alliance in Oklahoma City (which has an estimated 1,200 to 1,500 homeless residents), ideas about housing the homeless are changing. He says that the old model is based on a continuum of care that begins in an emergency homeless shelter, where the newly homeless get shelter, food, clothing, and access to government and nonprofit services. Those ready to move on typically go to transitional housing and then to permanent housing, often with financial support.

However, many communities, notably large metropolitan areas on the East and West coasts, have taken a different tack in the last five to 10 years. Their approach, called "housing first," moves the homeless person into supportive housing immediately. The aim is to get homeless individuals off the streets and into a self-supportive culture that will keep them housed and self-reliant.

A day in supportive housing costs significantly less than a day in jail or in a psychiatric hospital, and . . . even less than a day in a shelter.

"The thought is that it's a lot more likely that a person will work on their problems if they're in an apartment or single-room occupancy facility rather than in a cavernous barracks with 100 other people with the same and worse problems," explains Straughan. "Some really good longitudinal research indicates that this approach can be both cost-effective and successful."

He cites a study by the Lewin Group, a national health care and human services consulting firm based in Falls

Church, Virginia, which examined the daily cost of supportive housing in nine cities: San Francisco, Los Angeles, Atlanta, New York, Chicago, Boston, Seattle, Phoenix, and Columbus, Ohio. The results of the study, issued in November 2004, showed that a day in supportive housing costs significantly less than a day in jail or in a psychiatric hospital, and a day in permanent supportive housing costs even less than a day in a shelter.

The Fannie Mae Foundation and the Corporation for Supportive Housing, a nonprofit based in New Haven, Connecticut, followed 4,679 people placed in supportive housing and found that their total annual unit costs were $17,277—or nearly $6,000 less than it takes to house an individual in a shelter, according to figures compiled by the New York-based Coalition for the Homeless.

"A formerly homeless person in stable housing is twice as likely to be employed," says Straughan, "twice as likely to be physically and mentally healthy, to be free from substance abuse, and to stay out of jail, than a homeless person either in the shelter system or on the street."

Portland, Oregon, is one city that is embracing the housing first approach. In a report issued December 2004, *Home Again: A Ten Year Plan to End Homelessness in Portland and Multnomah County*, the city states that "the most critical issue that faces all homeless people—the lack of permanent housing—will be addressed first. Other services and programs directed at homeless people and families will support and maintain homeless people in this permanent housing."

In the midst of the current real estate bubble, more and more families are becoming homeless.

The report sets an ambitious goal for the city and county: to create 2,200 new permanent supportive housing units for chronically homeless individuals and homeless families with special needs by the year 2015.

To accomplish these goals, the city will focus on three specific areas: First, it will attend to the problems of the most chronically homeless. Then it will streamline access to existing services in an effort to prevent further homelessness—for example, by seeking more partnerships with nonprofits. Finally, it will put resources into specific programs that offer measurable results.

The Emerging Homeless

In the midst of the current real estate bubble, more and more families are becoming homeless, says Joan Noguera, executive director of the Nassau-Suffolk Coalition for the Homeless on Long Island—the suburban area east of New York City. "We have a housing market that has gone sky high," she says.

She points out that Long Islanders have a median income of $85,000, yet many wage earners don't earn 30 percent of that figure. The region is home to some of the nation's most affluent communities, but some 40,000 individuals are homeless. Two-thirds of those are members of families; half are children. According to data released by the Urban Institute in 2000, children make up about 39 percent of the homeless population nationally.

Noguera cites an example of a single mother with children who is currently in a homeless shelter and is seeking a rental unit for $900 per month—hard to find on suburban Long Island. To secure an apartment, she needs the first month's rent plus two months' security deposit—or $2,700. The coalition was trying to help her, but without the funds, she and her children would remain in a shelter.

Families composed 41 percent of the urban homeless population, according to a U.S. Conference of Mayors survey completed in 2004. This was an increase of five percent over the two previous years. "The face of homelessness has changed," said James Garner, mayor of the village of Hemp-stead, Long Island, when the survey was released. Garner is a past president of the mayors' conference.

Advocates for the homeless agree that services are crucial.

New York as a whole seems to be on the right track. Linda Gibbs, commissioner of the city's Department of Homeless Services, recently announced that from December 2004 to May of [2005], the number of people in the city's homeless shelters dropped by 2,379 individuals, the largest decline in any six-month period since 1990. The number of homeless children dropped by 13 percent, from 15,766 in May 2004 to 13,770 in May 2005. These results put the city ahead of an aggressive target set by Mayor Michael Bloomberg to reduce homelessness by two-thirds over a five-year period.

Services Are Crucial

"In my view, large-scale homelessness of the kind we have seen over the past 25 years is primarily attributable to the policy of deinstitutionalizing the mentally ill," says Seth Forman, AICP [American Institute of Certified Planners], deputy director of the Long Island Regional Planning Board. Forman believes that homelessness has less to do with housing markets than with poor mental health, addiction, and physical abuse.

Advocates for the homeless agree that services are crucial. That means services to enhance life skills and budgeting skills and rehabilitation for drugs and alcohol. Affordable housing without such services is not likely to work, the experts say.

Father Joe's Villages, a faith-based nonprofit organization in San Diego, follows that premise. Its founder, Father Joe Carroll, won the American Planning Association's Paul David-off Award for advocacy in 1997. The organization's innovative formula for programs and services has been endorsed as a prototype by the Department of Housing and Urban Development.

A recent project developed by Father Joe's Villages is Villa Harvey Mandel, opened in May 2003. It is a $13.3 million, six-story affordable housing development with 90 units that provides a home to the "hardest-to-serve" community members, with residents ranging from the extremely low-income and formerly homeless to those with chronic physical disabilities, substance abuse problems, and mental illness. The project was awarded the "2004 Special Needs Housing Project of the Year" by the San Diego Housing Federation.

Units vary in size from 326-square-foot studios to 540-square-foot one bedrooms, with many of the west-facing apartments offering views of the Coronado Bridge, Petco Park, and downtown San Diego. The development also features the world's largest glass mosaic, titled "Neighbors Helping Neighbors: A Tribute to Donors, Volunteers, and Staff."

Support services are offered at the nearby St. Vincent de Paul Village, also affiliated with Father Joe's Villages. Services include medical and dental care, counseling, job training and placement services, legal assistance, information and referral, and assistance with entitlement programs.

Eight of the units at Villa Harvey Mandel are designated Shelter Plus Care units for formerly homeless single adults with disabilities. Some 25 beds are reserved for single adults who have mental illness or are chemically dependent. At the time of application, all prospective special needs residents must complete a certification form verifying their disability or special needs. Many residents are both substance abusers and have a mental illness.

Getting project approval wasn't easy. To combat negative perceptions, Father Joe's Villages met many times with East Village and Barrio Logan groups. The city council approved the project by a single vote. Construction began in April 2002.

Obstacles to Housing the Homeless

Permit processing for affordable housing is her agency's biggest headache when it comes to dealing with homelessness, says Marcella Escobar, deputy director of San Diego's Development Services, a branch of the city's planning department. "Fast tracking the permit process has been the focus that our department has taken. We realize that time is of the essence," she says.

That's where the affordable housing expediting program comes in. "In the past we had situations where [permitting] would take six months to a year, if not longer," Escobar says. With the expediting program, some projects have received discretionary approvals and gotten to a public hearing within three months, she adds.

The city of San Diego works hand in hand with various social organizations and community and faith-based groups to assist the city's homeless population. It is also renowned for developing single-room-occupancy housing—the type of housing that can prevent homelessness because the units are affordable to people with very modest incomes.

Bureaucracy is the enemy of housing solutions.

Community Housing Works, a local nonprofit organization near San Diego, is mindful of the problems caused by the not-in-my-backyard syndrome. Sue Reynolds, the organization's executive director, says her group works with the surrounding community through a board of directors that includes local residents, businesses, and government officials.

One of the group's projects, the Marisol Apartments in Oceanside, California, won APA's [American Planning Association's] Paul Davidoff Award in 1999. Everyone living in the 21 apartments there is HIV-symptomatic or has AIDS. Ten apartments are reserved for the homeless. Rents range from about $110 to $300 a month, and the apartments serve residents with monthly incomes of $330 to $1,000.

The project wasn't greeted with universal approval, Reynolds says, but her group used what she calls "old-fashioned community work" to turn the tide. It managed to convince neighbors that the new project would be better than what it was replacing.

"In many communities, the faith-based community is doing the lion's share of the day-to-day work with the homeless," says Dan Straughan. "The nonprofit community is also deeply involved. It behooves a city planning department to become (or get access to) a community convenor—that is, an organization that can bring many groups together to reach a consensus on how to best attack a problem."

A last word from Straughan: Bureaucracy is the enemy of housing solutions, which face what he calls the three Bs of homeless funding: "It's byzantine in its complexity, burdensome in the amount of oversight required to administer, and blind to local community need."

Youth Homelessness Is a Serious Problem

National Alliance to End Homelessness

The National Alliance to End Homelessness is a nonpartisan, mission-driven organization committed to preventing and ending homelessness in the United States.

Youth homelessness is disturbingly common. Although the prevalence of youth homelessness is difficult to measure, researchers estimate that about 5 to 7.7 percent of youth— about 1 million to 1.6 million youth per year—experience homelessness.

Homelessness has serious consequences for youth. It is especially dangerous for youth between the ages of 16 and 24 who do not have familial support. Living in shelters or on the streets, unaccompanied homeless youth are at a higher risk for physical and sexual assault or abuse and physical illness, including HIV/AIDS. It is estimated that 5,000 unaccompanied youth die each year as a result of assault, illness, or suicide. Furthermore, homeless youth are at a higher risk for anxiety disorders, depression, post-traumatic stress disorder, and suicide due to increased exposure to violence while living on their own. Homeless youth are also more likely to become involved in prostitution, to use and abuse drugs, and to engage in other dangerous and illegal behaviors.

This brief reviews the key issues surrounding youth homelessness, including causes and characteristics of homeless youth. It will also explain the youth housing continuum, a model to develop stable, supportive housing to prevent and end youth homelessness in America. For purposes of the brief, the definition of homeless youth includes any youth between

National Alliance to End Homelessness, "Fundamental Issues to Prevent and End Youth Homelessness," *Youth Homelessness Series Brief No. 1*, May 2006. Reproduced by permission.

the ages of 16 and 24 who do not have familial support and are unaccompanied—living in shelters or on the street.

The phenomenon of youth homelessness is largely a reflection of family dysfunction and breakdown.

The Causes of Youth Homelessness

Although the causes for homelessness among youth vary greatly by individual, the underlying themes among these causes reveal a strong link between homelessness and broader social issues including:

Family Breakdown. The same factors that contribute to adult homelessness such as poverty, lack of affordable housing, low education levels, unemployment, mental health, and substance abuse issues can also play a role in the occurrence and duration of a youth's homelessness. Beyond those factors, the phenomenon of youth homelessness is largely a reflection of family dysfunction and breakdown, specifically familial conflict, abuse, and disruption.

Youth usually enter a state of homelessness as a result of:

- Running away from home;

- Being locked out or abandoned by their parents or guardians; or

- Running or being emancipated or discharged from institutional or other state care.

Although family conflict also plays a part in adult homelessness, the nexus is more critical for youth since they are, by virtue of their developmental stage in life, still largely financially, emotionally, and, depending on their age, legally dependent upon their families.

Systems Failure. In addition, many youth become homeless due to systems failure of mainstream programs like child welfare, juvenile corrections, and mental health programs. Every year between 20,000 and 25,000 youth ages 16 and older transition from foster care to legal emancipation, or "age out" of the system. They enter into society with few resources and numerous challenges. As a result, former foster care children and youth are disproportionately represented in the homeless population. Twenty-five percent of former foster youth nationwide reported that they had been homeless at least one night within two-and-a-half to four years after exiting foster care.

Many youth encounter the juvenile justice system while homeless. Without a home, family support, or other resources, homeless youth are often locked up because they are without supervision. Homeless youth are socially marginalized and often arrested for "status" offenses—an action that is only illegal when performed by minors, like running away or breaking curfew. For youth who are released from juvenile corrections facilities, reentry is often difficult because they lack the familial support systems and opportunities for work and housing. Additionally, homeless youth are more likely than the general youth population to become involved in the juvenile justice system.

Characteristics of Homeless Youth

While the youth population is extremely diverse, a review of the research tells us that there are certain similarities among homeless youth, including:

Homeless youth are at a higher risk for anxiety disorders, depression, post-traumatic stress disorder, and suicide.

Lack of Self-Sufficiency Skills. Unlike adults who have often lived independently prior to experiencing homelessness, most youth who become homeless have never lived on their own.

Lacking financial means, marketable skills, maturity, and independent living skills, this is a task for which they are almost invariably ill prepared.

Lack of Financial Resources. Minimal education attainment and lack of job skills prevent most homeless youth from securing more than low-wage and short term jobs. Many youth are not able to sustain stable housing, much less cover other necessities such as food, clothing, and health care.

Mental Health and Post-Traumatic Stress Disorder. Homeless youth are at a higher risk for anxiety disorders, depression, post-traumatic stress disorder, and suicide due to increased exposure to violence while living on their own. Homeless young people have high rates of physical and sexual abuse. Approximately 40 to 60 percent experience physical abuse and between 17 and 35 percent experience sexual abuse. Due to their emotional and financial exploitability, homeless youth are especially vulnerable to coercion and recruitment into "survival sex"—the exchange of sex for survival needs such as food, shelter, gifts, money, or drugs.

Physical Health. Chronic health conditions, including asthma, other lung problems, high blood pressure, tuberculosis, diabetes, hepatitis, or HIV/AIDS are prevalent among homeless youth. Homeless young people over the age of 18 report that health care bills contribute to their inability to obtain stable housing. Youth are less likely to access health care services due to barriers like limited shelter placement, lack of health insurance, fear of shelters and health care providers, and distrust of highly structured, rule-bound programs.

Substance Abuse. According to national surveys, 75 percent of street youths were using marijuana, about 33 percent were using hallucinogens, stimulants, and analgesics, and 25 percent were using crack, other forms of cocaine, inhalants, and sedatives. Substance abuse rates vary greatly among homeless youth according to gender, age, ethnicity, and current living situations. Street youth have the highest rates of substance use and abuse, followed by sheltered youth and runaways, and then housed youth. These rates often increase with age.

Relationships and Social Networks

Homeless young people often seek relationships and social networks for support and survival. Some deal with their social marginalization by connecting with others on the street. Certain young people may look to familial support from grandparents or siblings for emotional and informational support, such as having someone to share and understand feelings with or being offered advice, information, or guidance. Some older teens will choose to sleep on couches or in spare bedrooms of friends, if only for a day or month at a time, to avoid sleeping on the street. Others will attempt to establish strong relationships with older adults who work within the programs from which they receive services.

It is often these relationships that can prevent homelessness. For example, a trusted advisor or friend can influence and motivate a youth to stay in or access stable housing. Young people who are able to stay in the same community or in the same schools as before they became homeless have a better chance of avoiding the dangerous consequences for youth who do not have familiar support. Yet, many young people find themselves homeless after exhausting all their resources and relationships with people and organizations who could help them access or prevent them from losing stable housing.

In summary, the causes of youth homelessness often include family breakdown and system failure. Many youth become homeless after running away from home, being locked out or abandoned by their parents or guardians, and running or being emancipated or discharged from institutional and other state care. As a consequence of being homeless, many youth lack self-sufficiency skills and financial resources. Most likely, homeless young people will suffer from mental health disorders, including post-traumatic stress disorder and substance abuse disorders, and have poor physical health and limited access to quality healthcare. Relationships and social networks are very important to the support and survival of homeless youth. Most importantly, strong and positive relationships with adults, programs, or organizations can prevent a homeless episode.

Communities should work to ensure young people—like those transitioning out of the foster care system and those leaving juvenile corrections—have safe, stable and affordable housing options. Strategies should include housing linked with service delivery models. Across the nation, communities must seek to understand and tailor solutions to the unique needs of homeless youth—only then can we prevent and end youth homelessness.

Poverty in the United States Is Not a Big Problem

Robert Rector, interviewed by Bill Steigerwald

Robert Rector is a senior research fellow at the Heritage Foundation, a conservative think tank. Bill Steigerwald is a columnist at The Pittsburgh Tribune-Review.

Robert Rector of The Heritage Foundation is a national authority on poverty and the U.S. welfare system. Specializing in welfare reform and family breakdown, Rector has done extensive research on the economic and social costs of welfare.

With presidential candidates of a certain hue decrying the suffering of the 37 million Americans who have been officially classified as poor by the U.S. Census Bureau, we thought we'd ask Rector if these poor people are really as poverty-stricken as we have been led to believe. I talked to the author of "America's Failed $5.4 Trillion War on Poverty" Thursday, Sept. 6 [2007,] by telephone from his office in Washington:

Bill Steigerwald: John Edwards and others lament that 37 million Americans struggle with incredible poverty every day. You say it is not so simple or accurate to think of them as truly poor. What do you mean?

Robert Rector: Well, when John Edwards says that one in eight Americans do not have enough money for food, shelter or clothing, that's generally what the average citizen is thinking about when they hear the word "poverty." But if that's what we mean by poverty, then virtually none of these 37 million people that are ostensibly poor are actually poor. In reality, the government runs multiple surveys that allow us to examine the physical living conditions of these individuals in great detail.

When you look at the people who John Edwards insists are poor, what you find is that the overwhelming majority of them have cable television, have air conditioning, have microwaves, have two color TVs; 45 percent of them own their own homes, which are typically three-bedroom homes with 1 1/2 baths in very good condition. On average, poor people who live in either apartments or in houses are not crowded and actually have more living space than the average person living in European countries, such as France, Italy or England.

Also, a lot of people believe that poor people are malnourished. But in fact when you look at the average nutriment intake of poor children, it is virtually indistinguishable from upper-middle-class children. In fact, poor kids by the time they reach age 18 or 19 are taller and heavier than the average middle-class teenagers in the 1950s at the time of Elvis. And the boys, when they reach 18, are a full one inch taller and 10 pounds heavier than the GIs [U.S. soldiers] storming the beaches of Normandy. It's pretty hard to accomplish that if you are facing chronic food shortages throughout your life.

The Truly Poor

How many Americans would you define as "truly poor"?

If you are looking at people who do not have adequate warm, dry apartments that are in good repair, and don't have enough food to feed their kids, you're probably looking at one family in 100, not one family in eight.

Who are these "truly poor" and where do they live?

Generally, they will be families that have a whole lot of behavioral issues in addition to mere economic issues—possibly drug problems, mental problems, certainly very low work effort, probably unmarried mothers and so forth. They would be spread around the country. Very few of them are elderly. Even though the elderly appear to have low incomes, they are not likely to lack food or to have a hole in their roof or things like that.

Is there any single reason why the "official poor" are poor?

If you look at the official poor, particularly at children who are officially in poverty, there are two main reasons for that. One is that their parents don't work much. Typically in a year, poor families with children will have about 16 hours of adult work per week in the household. If you raised that so that you had just one adult working full time, 75 percent of those kids would immediately be raised out of poverty.

Close to two-thirds of all poor children live in single-parent families.

The second major reason that children are poor is a single parenthood in the absence of marriage. Close to two-thirds of all poor children live in single-parent families. What we find is that if a never-married mother married the father of her children, again, about 70 percent of them would immediately be raised out of poverty. Most of these men who are fathers without being married in fact have jobs and have a fairly good capacity to support a family.

Counting the Poor

How many of those 37 million are children—and why do they count them as poor people?

They are counted as part of the household—what they judge is the whole household's income. Part of the reason the Census Bureau is telling us that we have 37 million poor people is that it judges families to be poor if they have incomes roughly less than $20,000 a year. But it doesn't count virtually any welfare income as income. So food stamps, public housing, Medicaid—all of the $600 billion that we spend assisting poor people (per year) is not counted as income when they go to determine whether a family is poor.

Are these 37 million officially poor people the same people year after year, decade after decade?

Not exactly. Some of them are just down there temporarily. Others tend to be in poor or near-poor status for a long time. That would tend to be true of single mothers, for example.... But vis-a-vis the single mothers, it's important to understand that 38 percent of all children are born to a mother who is not married and in half of the cases she is actually living with the father and the couple will express an interest in marriage but it never actually happens. One of the simplest and most important things we could do to reduce child poverty would be to go and communicate to those couples—all of whom are low-income—the importance of marriage for their own well-being and for the child's well-being.

The politically correct thing to do is to just exaggerate the amount of poverty that exists in the United States as a way of encouraging more welfare spending.

You don't make these numbers up—you rely on information provided by the Census Bureau. So how does this myth of the poor never seem to be debunked or straightened out in the media?

All of the data I provide come directly from government surveys. Those government surveys are not heavily publicized by the media, because since the beginning of the War on Poverty [declared by President Lyndon Johnson in 1964] the politically correct thing to do is to just exaggerate the amount of poverty that exists in the United States as a way of encouraging more welfare spending.

Welfare Spending on the Poor

You said we're spending $600 billion a year?

That's what we are spending on cash, food, housing and medical care. The biggest program in there is Medicaid, followed by something called the "earned income tax credit." The federal government, with state governments, runs 70 different means-tested welfare programs. These are programs that provide assistance exclusively to poor and low-income Americans.

How much of this money actually gets to the poor people who need it and how much is overhead?

Most of the money goes directly to poor people either as services or as something like a food stamp or medical care. The problem with these programs is that they reward individuals for not working and not being married. Essentially, they set up a very negative set of incentives that tends to push people deeper into poverty rather than helping them climb out of it.

The problem with the welfare state is not that it has huge overhead costs. In fact, the overhead costs are only about 15 percent of total costs. The problem is that aid is given in such a way that it encourages dependence rather than helping people to become self-sufficient.

We have spent a lot of money but we spent money in such a way that we displaced the work effort of the poor.

Dependency on Welfare

I've read that the national poverty rate declined steadily until it hit about 13 percent in about 1965. It's been stuck there since, despite trillions of dollars in welfare spending. Is this true—and why?

Yes. Poverty was declining rapidly before the War on Poverty was created in the mid-1960s, and since that time the poverty rate has basically stagnated. There are two reasons for that. One is that none of the poverty spending is counted as income, so that it can't have an anti-poverty effect. But the second, more important reason is that all of these programs discourage work and marriage, so that they in fact are pushing people deeper into poverty at the same time that they are giving them aid.

So it is true that the official poverty rate is stuck at about 12 or 13 percent?

It hasn't varied terribly much since the beginning of the War on Poverty.

Despite how many trillions being spent?

Since the beginning of the War on Poverty we have now spent over 11 trillion dollars.

Where did that money go—and who got it?

Basically, we have spent a lot of money but we spent money in such a way that we displaced the work effort of the poor, so that we did not get very much net increase in income. Rather than bringing people's incomes up, what we've done is supplanted work with welfare. What you need to do in order to truly get improvements is to create a welfare system that requires work and encourages marriage so that the recipient is moving toward self-sufficiency while receiving aid, rather than receiving aid in lieu of his own work efforts.

We've known for a long time about these problems with the welfare system. Is there any progress being made to fix them?

In 1996, we reformed one small welfare program—Aid to Families with Dependent Children—by requiring the recipients or part of the recipients to perform work in exchange for the benefits.

As a result of that, we got a huge decline in welfare rolls, a huge surge in employment and record drops in black child poverty. Unfortunately, the rest of the welfare system—the remaining 69 programs—remained unreformed. Until we reform those programs in a similar way, we will make no further progress against poverty.

Poverty in the United States Is Usually Short Lived

George B. Weathersby

George B. Weathersby is founder, chairman, and CEO of Genesys Solutions, a management consulting firm.

Four decades after President Lyndon Johnson declared war on poverty in 1964 it remains a compelling need in America. The US Census Bureau still measures poverty in great detail, and the total number of people living in poverty during each of the past 40 years has remained stubbornly high. After hundreds of billions of dollars have been spent to aid impoverished Americans, the conventional wisdom is that more than 35 million are still without adequate income.

Conventional wisdom describes the "poor" as a large and persistent group of families and individuals left out of the economic success of America. Enduring debilitating poverty, the poor—a group of individuals larger than California's entire population—are entitled to political advocates, specially funded programs, and government bureaucracies to coordinate benefits.

Fortunately for America, the basic description of the poor is wrong. And therefore public policy based upon an aggregate view of poverty is inherently misinformed. A closer look at the facts shows a different picture.

The Census Bureau and other researchers have been studying people and their families as they enter poverty, cope with the difficult challenges of poverty, and rise out of poverty as successful wage earners.

There are two basic areas of knowledge that offer the greatest illumination to our understanding of poverty in America:

George B. Weathersby, "The War on Poverty: Most of the 'Poor' in the U.S. Are Not Poor for Long," *Christian Science Monitor*, May 22, 2006, p. 9. Reproduced by permission of the author.

(1) The dynamics of poverty—how people enter poverty and exit poverty and how long people remain in poverty; and (2) the trigger points that cause people to become poor and the additional trigger points that enable people to rise out of poverty.

Unlike most other developed nations, poverty in America is a transitional process.

The basic facts are that while millions of people enter poverty (primarily because of a loss of a job or a family breakup) each year, most people remain poor for less than 5 months, and millions of people reenter the labor force and earn enough to rise above poverty. For two-thirds of people in poverty the transition in and out of poverty is relatively quick. For others, especially single parents with small children and the elderly beyond the work force, poverty is persistent for a number of years.

A Transitional Phase

The Panel for the Study of Income Dynamics has shown that the number of people who enter and leave poverty each year from the mid-1970s through the mid-1990s was about 8 million. Sometimes this number rose to nearly 20 million people entering and rising out of poverty in a single year. The description of a stable group of people who are poor, with a few becoming poor and a few rising out of poverty each year, is wildly wrong.

Every five years during the past three decades, between 30 million and 40 million Americans have risen out of poverty. This is an enormous accomplishment for the individuals, their families, and the caring society that has supported them. Unfortunately, every five years during the past three decades almost as many people have entered poverty for one or more reasons. But unlike most other developed nations, poverty in

America is a transitional process—from acceptable income levels into poverty and back to acceptable income again. Typically, this is a quick transition.

In a 1998 report, the Census Bureau carefully studied a sample of individuals who were poor from October 1992 through 1995. During this time, the overall annual poverty rate was 12.6 percent to 12.9 percent, almost identical to the 12.7 percent annual poverty rate in 2004. In 1994, 6.9 million people who were not poor in 1993 became poor sometime during the year. During the same year, 7.6 million people who were poor at the end of 1993 rose out of poverty during 1994. The net change was 700,000 fewer people in poverty at the end of 1994 than at the end of 1993, resulting in a small reduction in the annual poverty rate.

In addition to observing that 10 times as many people actually rose out of poverty than the net change in the poverty level in 1994, the Census Bureau also measured the actual number of months each person earned less than the poverty level of income. The mean period that all individuals who were poor sometime in 1993 or 1994 actually lived below the poverty level was 4.5 months. Half of all individuals who were poor at any time in 1993 or 1994 were poor for less than 4.5 months. Yes, children were poor longer: 5.3 months at the median. And households headed by females were poor longer: 7.2 months.

About one-third of individuals who were poor in the beginning of 1993 remained poor for 24 months or more. The persistent poverty rate in 1994 was 5.3 percent versus an average poverty rate of 15.4 percent (and an annual poverty rate of 12.9 percent).

Differing Policies

The policy implications of these dynamics, and the actual trigger events, are significant. To accelerate the transition out of poverty, government agencies need to qualify applicants and deliver services within weeks of entering poverty or the public expenditures will be largely irrelevant. Long-term support issues of housing, training, and education may be important to the one-third chronically poor, but not to the two-thirds in transit through poverty.

The war on poverty needs to be fought on at least two fronts. First is the quick response, transactional battle of month to month for those at the edge of poverty to sustain or regain employment and family stability—supporting most of the people and most cost-effective support because it leverages their own substantial family and financial momentum. The second is the chronic poor, where there is a different strategy of long-term support and gradual transition.

As the 1998 Census Bureau report concluded, "Poverty may seem to be a relatively simple picture, but, in fact, it is complex."

Homelessness Is Declining

Kevin Fagan

Kevin Fagan is a reporter who covers homelessness issues for The San Francisco Chronicle.

Three years after the [2003] launch of the most aggressive nationwide strategy in a generation to solve homelessness, there is evidence that it may be working: The number of street people in cities across the United States has plummeted for the first time since the 1980s.

The drop-off reflected in street counts of the homeless taken over [2005] has ranged from 30 percent in Miami and 28 percent in Dallas to 20 percent in Portland, Ore., and 13 percent in New York. In all, 30 jurisdictions reported declines in their homeless populations, including the 28 percent dip recorded in San Francisco [in mid-2005] and a 4 percent drop reported [in mid-2006] in Denver.

The figures emerged as more than 250 civic and social program leaders—all of whom are behind 10-year plans to end chronic homelessness across the nation—gathered in Denver to compare notes for the first time since the [George W.] Bush administration began pushing for creation of the plans in 2003. They all agreed on at least two things.

One, they need more funding, especially at a time when federal allocations to fight poverty overall—such as Section 8 vouchers that help the poor with partial rent payments—are dipping. But they also agreed that even in that tough economic climate, the 216 cities and counties and 53 states and territories that are pursuing 10-year plans seem to be making headway toward easing the nation's homelessness crisis by focusing more tightly on the most pressing problems.

The plummeting homeless counts, taken in one-day tallies in shelters and streets at varying dates across the country, are "not an aberration," Philip Mangano, executive director of the U.S. Interagency Council on Homelessness, said in an address to the National Summit for Jurisdictional Leaders. "They are part of a national trend.

"So does this mean we have done enough?" [asked] Mangano, President Bush's point man on the issue.

"No. But are we doing better? Absolutely."

The Chronic Homeless

The goal of the 10-year plans is to put the most dysfunctional homeless people in the country—that 10 percent to 20 percent who are continually on the street with addiction or mental problems—quickly into permanent "supportive" housing with counseling services to help them get healthy. Those chronic cases are a tremendous financial burden on their communities in hospital, jail and other services—hundreds of thousands of dollars apiece annually in some instances.

The savings from stabilizing these hard-core homeless people in more cost-effective supportive housing can be used to extend services to all the homeless, say Mangano and other proponents of the plans.

Putting teeth into the Bush administration's promotion of the concept, agencies awarding federal homeless grants in the past three years have begun favoring communities that have 10-year plans in place.

The last time there was such a widespread national strategy to address homelessness was in the mid-1980s, when cities from San Francisco to New York built shelters and systems to route people into health services so they could eventually move into residences. That method has been widely discredited since the late 1990s as social scientists determined that a $12,000-a-year supportive housing unit is more cost-effective than a $35,000-a-year shelter bed.

Critics of the Strategy Focus

While lauding the 10-year planning concept, however, some among the mayors, governors, welfare directors and social agency workers who came to discuss their efforts cautiously complained that focusing on the more hard-core people is neglecting the plight of homeless families. In some communities, such as New York or Contra Costa County [California], families constitute at least half of the homeless population. In San Francisco, they constitute up to 20 percent.

Mangano touted the Bush administration's allocation of more than $4 billion [in 2006] in funds targeted for the homeless—a 7 percent increase over [2005]—but the leaders and social-program directors gathered in Denver said they feared that cuts in other anti-poverty health and housing programs might leave them running in place.

The criticism is echoed by homeless advocacy groups, including the National Coalition for the Homeless, which remains skeptical that homelessness overall is actually declining.

"The 10-year plans are an excellent step forward, but at the same time we need to remember the existing needs of everyone, to not cannibalize other funding while we do this thing for the chronics," Zach Krochina, the coalition's economic justice policy coordinator, said in a phone interview from Washington.

This was the first time since the beginning of the nation's homelessness crisis in the early 1980s that . . . a mass of cities report[ed] a simultaneous decrease in street population rather than an increase.

University of Pennsylvania Professor Dennis Culhane, a leading researcher on the benefits of supportive housing, said he could understand the concerns. But concentrating efforts on the chronic cases will pay off for everyone in the end, he insisted.

Doing What Works

"We have a solution that we know works, and we shouldn't take our eyes off that," Culhane said at one of the sessions at [May 2006's] three-day gathering. . . . "We can't do everything at once. We can't get distracted. Be patient."

Each city's homelessness count is done on its own time and in its own way, and there is no central collection point of data for such counts. But Mangano and the others convened in Denver—some of whom included homeless street advocates who several years ago were loudly skeptical of almost anything governmental—agreed this was the first time since the beginning of the nation's homelessness crisis in the early 1980s that they could remember a mass of cities reporting a simultaneous decrease in street population rather than an increase.

"It really seems there was a paradigm shift a couple of years ago," said John Parvensky, president of Colorado Coalition for the Homeless, who used to protest governmental inaction on the street crisis but today helps guide Denver's 10-year plan.

"People like Mark Trotz began showing that you can't just spend all your time getting people ready for housing by trying to clean them up first or keep them forever in shelters," Parvensky said, referring to initiatives led by the director of homeless housing for San Francisco's Department of Public Health. "You have to house them first. And that has changed everything."

San Francisco has been particularly innovative in this regard, Mangano told the meeting attendees—so much so that former Supervisor Angela Alioto received a newly created "City Champion Award" from the Interagency Council for overseeing the creation of San Francisco's 10-Year Plan to Abolish Chronic Homelessness in 2004.

"San Francisco, like many other cities, had been a case study for 20 years in zigzagging on the problem, lurching from tactic to tactic every few years," said Trotz, who oversees

Direct Access to Housing, a city program lauded and copied all over the country for its success in housing and counseling severely disabled homeless people. "But now we think we know what works—housing first, supportive housing.

"And the limited success we're seeing now is a testament to staying the course."

CHAPTER 2

What Causes Poverty and Homelessness?

Chapter Preface

There are numerous theories about the causes of poverty and homelessness, and it is quite likely that for any one person suffering from these conditions, multiple causes come into play. Determining the causes of poverty and homelessness is important in order to address the problem and to find effective, long-term solutions. While homeless shelters and affordable permanent housing address the immediate needs of people who are homeless, they may be ineffective in the long run if the causes of homelessness are not understood. If substance abuse, for example, is a primary cause of a person's homelessness, providing housing may not keep that individual off the streets if the addiction is not addressed. Thus, long-range solutions to both homelessness and poverty involve determining the causes, rather than simply addressing immediate needs.

Some commentators have argued that untreated mental illness is one of the main causes of homelessness. The National Health Care for the Homeless Council cites mental illness as one of the contributing factors leading to homelessness; the council claims that 39 percent of the homeless have a mental health problem. Some experts have linked the increased number of homeless people in recent decades to the closing of state-funded mental institutions. The National Coalition for the Homeless, however, disagrees with that theory, claiming that a substantial number of mental patients were released in the 1950s and 1960s, whereas the homeless population started spiking in the 1980s.

The U.S. Interagency Council on Homelessness has spearheaded a program called America's Road Home: A Partnership to End Chronic Homelessness; this program aims to work with mayors of cities to support local solutions to ending chronic homelessness, a condition defined, according to the

National Alliance to End Homelessness, as "long-term or re-peated homelessness of a person with a disability." The National Coalition for the Homeless (NCH), however, objects to the federal government's use of the term "chronic homeless-ness," arguing that this term distorts the causes of homelessness that the NCH believes are "fundamentally economic and not medical in nature." In addition, the NCH believes that although rates of disabilities such as mental illness are high among homeless individuals, "they do not explain homeless-ness." The NCH is concerned that the government's focus on chronic homelessness—and its lack of understanding that the key causes of homelessness are economic—will exacerbate the problem of homelessness. The viewpoints in this chapter debate the causes of poverty and homelessness.

Racial Discrimination Contributes to the Problem of Poverty

Alan Jenkins

Alan Jenkins is executive director of The Opportunity Agenda, an organization that works across social justice issues to build public support for greater opportunity in America.

Our nation, at its best, pursues the ideal that what we look like and where we come from should not determine the benefits, burdens, or responsibilities that we bear in our society. Because we believe that all people are created equal in terms of rights, dignity, and the potential to achieve great things, we see inequality based on race, gender, and other social characteristics as not only unfortunate but unjust. The value of equality, democratic voice, physical and economic security, social mobility, a shared sense of responsibility for one another, and a chance to start over after misfortune or missteps—what many Americans call redemption—are the moral pillars of the American ideal of opportunity.

Many Americans of goodwill who want to reduce poverty believe that race is no longer relevant to understanding the problem, or to fashioning solutions for it. This view often reflects compassion as well as pragmatism. But we cannot solve the problem of poverty—or, indeed, be the country that we aspire to be—unless we honestly unravel the complex and continuing connection between poverty and race.

Since our country's inception, race-based barriers have hindered the fulfillment of our shared values and many of these barriers persist today. Experience shows, moreover, that

Alan Jenkins, "Inequality, Race, and Remedy," *The American Prospect*, vol. 18, no. 5, May 2007. Reproduced with permission from *The American Prospect*, 11 Beacon Street, Suite 1120, Boston, MA 02108.

reductions in poverty do not reliably reduce racial inequality, nor do they inevitably reach low-income people of color. Rising economic tides do not reliably lift all boats.

In 2000, after a decade of remarkable economic prosperity, the poverty rate among African Americans and Latinos taken together was still 2.6 times greater than that for white Americans. This disparity was stunning, yet it was the smallest difference in poverty rates between whites and others in more than three decades. And from 2001 to 2003, as the economy slowed, poverty rates for most communities of color increased more dramatically than they did for whites, widening the racial poverty gap. From 2004 to 2005, while the overall number of poor Americans declined by almost 1 million, to 37 million, poverty rates for most communities of color actually increased. Reductions in poverty do not inevitably close racial poverty gaps, nor do they reach all ethnic communities equally.

Persistent racial discrimination . . . while subtler than in past decades, continues to deny opportunity to millions of Americans.

Poor people of color are also increasingly more likely than whites to find themselves living in high-poverty neighborhoods with limited resources and limited options. An analysis by The Opportunity Agenda and the Poverty & Race Research Action Council found that while the percentage of Americans of all races living in high-poverty neighborhoods (those with 30 percent or more residents living in poverty) declined between 1960 and 2000, the racial gap grew considerably. Low-income Latino families were three times as likely as low-income white families to live in these neighborhoods in 1960, but 5.7 times as likely in 2000. Low-income blacks were 3.8 times more likely than poor whites to live in high-poverty neighborhoods in 1960, but 7.3 times more likely in 2000.

These numbers are troubling not because living among poor people is somehow harmful in itself, but because concentrated high-poverty communities are far more likely to be cut off from quality schools, housing, health care, affordable consumer credit, and other pathways out of poverty. And African Americans and Latinos are increasingly more likely than whites to live in those communities. Today, low-income blacks are more than three times as likely as poor whites to be in "deep poverty"—meaning below half the poverty line—while poor Latinos are more than twice as likely.

The Persistence of Discrimination

Modern and historical forces combine to keep many communities of color disconnected from networks of economic opportunity and upward mobility. Among those forces is persistent racial discrimination that, while subtler than in past decades, continues to deny opportunity to millions of Americans. Decent employment and housing are milestones on the road out of poverty. Yet these are areas in which racial discrimination stubbornly persists. While the open hostility and "Whites Only" signs of the Jim Crow era have largely disappeared, research shows that identically qualified candidates for jobs and housing enjoy significantly different opportunities depending on their race.

In one study, researchers submitted identical résumés by mail for more than 1,300 job openings in Boston and Chicago, giving each "applicant" either a distinctively "white-sounding" or "black-sounding" name—for instance, "Brendan Baker" versus "Jamal Jones." Résumés with white-sounding names were 50 percent more likely than those with black-sounding names to receive callbacks from employers. Similar research in California found that Asian American and, especially, Arab American résumés received the least-favorable treatment compared to other groups. In recent studies in Milwaukee and New York City, meanwhile, live "tester pairs" with comparable qualifications but of differing races tested not only the effect of race on job prospects but also the impact of an apparent criminal record. In Milwaukee, whites reporting a criminal record were more likely to receive a callback from employers than were blacks without a criminal record. In New York, Latinos and African Americans without criminal records received fewer callbacks than did similarly situated whites, and at rates comparable to whites with a criminal record.

Similar patterns hamper the access of people of color to quality housing near good schools and jobs. Research by the U.S. Department of Housing and Urban Development (HUD) shows that people of color receive less information from real-estate agents, are shown fewer units, and are frequently steered away from predominantly white neighborhoods. In addition to identifying barriers facing African Americans and Latinos, this research found significant levels of discrimination against Asian Americans, and that Native American renters may face the highest discrimination rates (up to 29 percent) of all.

This kind of discrimination is largely invisible to its victims, who do not know that they have received inaccurate information or been steered away from desirable neighborhoods and jobs. But its influence on the perpetuation of poverty is nonetheless powerful.

The Present Legacy

These modern discriminatory practices often combine with historical patterns. In New Orleans, for example, as in many other cities, low-income African Americans were intentionally concentrated in segregated, low-lying neighborhoods and public-housing developments at least into the 1960s. In 2005, when Hurricane Katrina struck and the levees broke, black neighborhoods were most at risk of devastation. And when HUD announced that it would close habitable public-housing developments in New Orleans rather than clean and reopen them, it was African Americans who were primarily prevented from returning home and rebuilding. This and other failures to rebuild and invest have exacerbated poverty—already at high levels—among these New Orleanians.

In the case of Native Americans, a quarter of whom are poor, our government continues to play a more flagrant role in thwarting pathways out of poverty. Unlike other racial and ethnic groups, most Native Americans are members of sovereign tribal nations with a recognized status under our Constitution. High levels of Native American poverty derive not only from a history of wars, forced relocations, and broken treaties by the United States but also from ongoing breaches of trust—like our government's failure to account for tens of billions of dollars that it was obligated to hold in trust for Native American individuals and families. After more than a decade of litigation, and multiple findings of governmental wrongdoing, the United States is trying to settle these cases for a tiny fraction of what it owes.

The trust-fund cases, of course, are just the latest in a string of broken promises by our government. But focusing as they do on dollars and cents, they offer an important window into the economic status that Native American communities and tribes might enjoy today if the U.S. government lived up to its legal and moral obligations.

Researchers ... have repeatedly found that the mainstream media depict poor people as people of color— primarily African Americans.

Meanwhile, the growing diversity spurred by new immigrant communities adds to the complexity of contemporary poverty. Asian American communities, for example, are culturally, linguistically, and geographically diverse, and they span a particularly broad socioeconomic spectrum.

Census figures from 2000 show that while one-third of Asian American families have annual incomes of $75,000 or more, one-fifth have incomes of less than $25,000. While the Asian American poverty rate mirrored that of the country as a whole, Southeast Asian communities reflected far higher levels. Hmong men experienced the highest poverty level (40.3 percent) of any racial group in the nation.

Race and Public Attitudes

Americans' complex attitudes and emotions about race are crucial to understanding the public discourse about poverty and the public's will to address it. Researchers such as Martin Gilens and Herman Gray have repeatedly found that the mainstream media depict poor people as people of color—primarily African Americans—at rates far higher than their actual representation in the population. And that depiction, the research finds, interacts with societal biases to erode support for antipoverty programs that could reach all poor people.

Gilens found, for instance, that while blacks represented only 29 percent of poor Americans at the time he did his research, 65 percent of poor Americans shown on television news were black. In a more detailed analysis of TV newsmagazines in particular, Gilens found a generally unflattering framing of the poor, but the presentation of poor African Americans was more negative still. The most "sympathetic" subgroups of the poor—such as the working poor and the elderly—were underrepresented on these shows, while unemployed working-age adults were overrepresented. And those disparities were greater for African Americans than for others, creating an even more unflattering (and inaccurate) picture of the black poor.

Gray similarly found that poor African Americans were depicted as especially dysfunctional and undeserving of assistance, with an emphasis on violence, poor choices, and dependency. As Gray notes, "The black underclass appears as a menace and a source of social disorganization in news accounts of black urban crime, gang violence, drug use, teenage pregnancy, riots, homelessness, and general aimlessness. In news accounts . . . poor blacks (and Hispanics) signify a social menace that must be contained."

Research also shows that Americans are more likely to blame the plight of poverty on poor people themselves, and less likely to support antipoverty efforts, when they perceive that the people needing help are black. These racial effects are especially pronounced when the poor person in the story is a black single mother. In one study, more than twice the number of respondents supported individual solutions (like the one that says poor people "should get a job") over societal solutions (such as increased education or social services) when the single mother was black.

We cannot hope to address poverty in a meaningful or lasting way without addressing race-based barriers to opportunity.

This research should not be surprising. [President] Ronald Reagan, among others, effectively used the "racialized" mental image of the African American "welfare queen" to undermine support for antipoverty efforts. And the media face of welfare recipients has long been a black one, despite the fact that African Americans have represented a minority of the welfare population. But this research also makes clear that unpacking and disputing racial stereotypes is important to rebuilding a shared sense of responsibility for reducing poverty in all of our communities.

Removing Racial Barriers

We cannot hope to address poverty in a meaningful or lasting way without addressing race-based barriers to opportunity. The most effective solutions will take on these challenges together.

That means, for example, job-training programs that prepare low-income workers for a globalized economy, combined with antidiscrimination enforcement that ensures equal access to those programs and the jobs to which they lead. Similarly, strengthening the right to organize is important in helping low-wage workers to move out of poverty, but it must be combined with civil-rights efforts that root out the racial exclusion that has sometimes infected union locals. And it means combining comprehensive immigration reform that offers newcomers a pathway to citizenship with living wages and labor protections that root out exploitation and discourage racial hierarchy.

Another crucial step is reducing financial barriers to college by increasing the share of need-based grants over student loans and better coordinating private-sector scholarship aid—for example, funds for federal Pell Grants should be at least double current levels. But colleges should also retain the flexibility to consider racial and socioeconomic background as two factors among many, in order to promote a diverse student body (as well as diverse workers and leaders once these students graduate). And Congress should pass the DREAM [Development, Relief and Education for Alien Minors] Act, which would clear the path to a college degree and legal immigration status for many undocumented students who've shown academic promise and the desire to contribute to our country. [The DREAM Act has not yet been passed, but was reintroduced to Congress in 2009.]

Lack of access to affordable, quality health care is a major stress on low-income families, contributing to half of the nation's personal bankruptcies. Guaranteed health care for all is critical, and it must be combined with protections against poor quality and unequal access that, research shows, affect people of color irrespective of their insurance status.

Finally, we must begin planning for opportunity in the way we design metropolitan regions, transportation systems, housing, hospitals, and schools. That means, for example, creating incentives for mixed-income neighborhoods that are well-publicized and truly open to people of all races and backgrounds.

Instead of balancing a list of constituencies and identity groups, our task becomes one of moving forward together as a diverse but cohesive society.

A particularly promising approach involves requiring an "opportunity impact statement" when public funds are to be used for development projects. The statement would explain, for example, whether a new highway will connect low-income communities to good jobs and schools, or serve only affluent communities. It would detail where and how job opportunities would flow from the project, and whether different communities would share the burden of environmental and other effects (rather than having the project reinforce traditional patterns of inequality). It would measure not only a project's expected effect on poverty but on opportunity for all.

When we think about race and poverty in terms of the shared values and linked fate of our people, our approach to politics as well as policy begins to change. Instead of balancing a list of constituencies and identity groups, our task becomes one of moving forward together as a diverse but cohesive society, addressing through unity the forces that have historically divided us.

The Absence of Fathers Causes Poverty

William Raspberry

William Raspberry is a retired Pulitzer Prize–winning Washington Post *columnist and professor emeritus at the Sanford Institute of Public Policy at Duke University.*

I first heard the numbers from sociologist Andrew Billingsley: In 1890, 80 percent of black American households were headed by husbands and wives. That's just 25 years after the end of the Civil War.

In 1900, the percentage was mostly unchanged, and so it remained—between the high 70s and the low 80s—for 1910, 1920, 1930, for every decennial census report until 1970, when it was down to 64.

For the 2000 Census, the percentage of black families headed by married couples was 38. The only good news is that it was also 38 percent in 1990, suggesting that the trend may have stopped getting worse.

More Likely to Be Poor

Now consider this: Fatherless families are America's single largest source of poverty. The Annie E. Casey Foundation's "Kids Count" once reported that Americans who failed to complete high school, to get married and to reach age 20 before having their first child were nearly 10 times as likely to live in poverty as those who did these three things.

Poverty, it goes without saying, is associated with poorer academic outcomes, which, in turn, are associated with poorer job prospects. That means, among other things, reduced ability to choose neighborhoods to bring children up in safety. Non-marriage has consequences.

Two things need to be said: The phenomenon obviously does not apply to all black families, nor is it *restricted* to black families. An impressive number of African Americans are succeeding beyond what earlier generations could even imagine (though I suspect that a disproportionate percentage of those outstanding successes are from two-parent families).

There's nothing inherently racial about the trend, of course. The 2000 Census showed that only 69 percent of all American children were born into two-parent households—65 percent for Hispanics and 77 percent for whites.

Further, fatherlessness does not affect all people equally. Whenever I address the topic, I am certain to hear from some people who want me to know that they were raised by a single mother and managed to turn out quite well, thank you. That doesn't surprise me, of course. There are children who are, for unexplained reasons, unusually resilient and self-motivated, and there are single mothers whose skill and discipline are so heroic that their children are virtually driven to succeed.

While marriage may not be a cure for poverty, it does turn out to be a fairly reliable preventative.

But acknowledging that "Peg Leg" Bates was a helluva tap dancer shouldn't obscure the fact that dancers are generally better off with the full complement of nether limbs.

Encourage Marriage

So am I urging all single mothers to grab the nearest adult male and haul him off to the altar?

Of course not. As Mary Frances Berry, then chair of the U.S. Commission on Civil Rights, once told me: "If all the single mothers in poor communities married single men in those same communities, and the men all moved in, the only effect would be to increase by one the number of disabled people in each household."

She was right, of course. But while marriage may not be a cure for poverty, it does turn out to be a fairly reliable *preventative*. Isn't it worthwhile to spend more time and resources helping young people to understand the economic implications of single parenthood *before* they become single parents? Wouldn't it make sense to rethink our relatively recent easy acceptance of out-of-wedlock parenting?

And might it not be a good idea to work at restoring the influence of the community institutions, religious and civic, that used to help strengthen families? The trends Billingsley talked about were a long time developing, and they won't be reversed in a day or two.

As he told me, "You can't have strong families unless you have strong communities, and you can't have strong communities unless you have strong institutions."

Phillip Jackson, executive director of Chicago's Black Star Project and promoter of the Million Father March, cites the oft-repeated proverb that it "takes a village to raise a child."

In too many parts of the black community, he said, "the proverb has little relevance. There is no village to raise the children . . . no collective community effort to ensure that most black children will grow up capable of succeeding in the 21st century.

"Unfortunately, African proverbs don't raise children. People do."

U.S. Anti-immigrant Policy Increases Poverty

Andres Oppenheimer

Andres Oppenheimer is the Latin American editor and syndicated foreign affairs columnist of The Miami Herald *and the author of* Saving the Americas.

If you were shocked by U.S. Census figures [of August 2007] showing that there are more than 36.5 million people living in poverty in the United States, get ready: It may get much worse in coming years!

Before I tell you why I fear that the gap between America's rich and poor is going to widen even more—courtesy of a majority of Republicans and some Democrats in the Senate who voted against an immigration reform bill what would have given a merit-based path to citizenship to many of the estimated 12 million undocumented U.S. residents—let's take a look at the alarming figures released [August 27, 2007]:

- The percentage of U.S. residents living below the poverty line dropped slightly [in 2006]. But the Center for American Progress, a group that defines itself as "progressive," points out that in absolute numbers the 36.5 million U.S. poor are nearly 5 million more than five years ago.

- The U.S. poverty rate is at 12.3 percent, a slight decrease from [2006's] but higher than five years ago, when it stood at 11.3 percent.

- The number of U.S. residents without healthcare coverage has reached 47 million, an increase of 8.5 million over the past five years. A sizable part of the U.S. population living below the poverty line or lacking medical insurance is Hispanic.

While poverty among Hispanics dropped slightly [in 2006], nearly 21 percent of U.S. Hispanics are still living in poverty, compared with about 8 percent of non-Hispanic whites, and about 10 percent of U.S. Asians. Only African Americans have higher poverty levels, with a 24 percent rate.

And Hispanics are by far the most likely to be uninsured: 34.1 percent of U.S. Hispanics lack medical coverage, compared with 20.5 percent of blacks and 14.9 percent of whites.

Poverty Will Get Worse

Why am I afraid that poverty levels will not drop anytime soon? First, the U.S. economy is slowing down. Some economic projections are already forecasting a meager 1.5 percent economic growth rate for 2008. That's likely to cost jobs.

Second, the recent defeat in the Senate of an immigration reform bill that would have offered a path to citizenship to millions of undocumented workers who learned English and paid fines, has resulted in a crackdown on unauthorized residents that will only help create an underclass of increasingly alienated—and poorer—Hispanic immigrants.

"Now, these people will not only remain underground, but will be less likely to learn English," says Michael Fix, of the Migration Policy Institute, a nonpartisan group. "It will keep the undocumented poor for a longer period of time."

Third, the [George W.] Bush administration, which has caved in to extremist anti-immigration groups and is now focusing on enforcement-only measures, recently said it will send letters to employers whose workers' Social Security numbers don't match government records. Under these rules, employers will have to lay off undocumented workers. And those who are laid off are not going to go home, nor stop having children.

"My guess is that people will go from one chicken processing plant to another, and their incomes may be reduced, and they may go through periods without income," says Cecilia Muñoz, of the National Council of La Raza, a Hispanic rights advocacy group. To make things worse, some [2008] presidential candidates, such as Republican Mitt Romney, are on a crusade against "illegal immigration," contributing—willingly or not—to a climate that encourages city ordinances across the country that bar undocumented workers from basic services.

Congress' failure to approve a path to citizenship . . . will send millions of Hispanics further underground, increasing America's overall poverty . . . rates.

My opinion: The last time the U.S. government gave a pathway to citizenship, in 1986, studies showed that the newly legalized citizens got better jobs soon afterward.

This time, thanks to a majority of Republicans who voted against immigration reform in the Senate and the Democrats who followed them, the U.S. Congress' failure to approve a path to citizenship will have the opposite effect: It will send millions of Hispanics further underground, increasing America's overall poverty and inequality rates.

Culture Contributes to the Cycle of Poverty

Cathy Young

Cathy Young is a contributing editor at Reason *magazine.*

After Hurricane Katrina and the devastation left in its wake exposed to public eye the shocking levels of poverty in the mostly African-American neighborhoods of New Orleans, there was a lot of talk about America's hidden shame and about the need to pay more attention to the plight of the poor when there isn't a natural disaster to put them in the headlines.

Just over a month later, the poor are off the front pages, and the press is far more interested in whether Harriet Miers is a deep legal thinker [Miers was nominated for the U.S. Supreme Court on Oct. 3, 2005, and then President George W. Bush withdrew her nomination on Oct. 27]. Meanwhile, the poor are always with us.

Part of the reason we don't talk much about poverty is that no one really knows what to do about it. Typically, the left wants to blame poverty on evil, racist Republicans and to advocate more redistribution of wealth and spending on social programs as the answer. Democratic congressman Charles Rangel of New York [has] stated that George W. Bush's inattention to poverty made him "our Bull Connor," comparing Bush to the 1960s Alabama police official whose name has become a symbol of racism.

The right, meanwhile, tends to blame bloated welfare programs for keeping the poor trapped in their condition, as well as the "culture of poverty" with its deeply entrenched social problems—which, all too often, translates into blaming the

Cathy Young, "The Problem of Poverty: Why Left and Right Have Little Serious to Say," *Reason Online*, October 18, 2005. www.reason.com. Reproduced by permission.

poor themselves. After the catastrophe in New Orleans, several conservative websites ran an article by Ayn Rand follower Robert Tracinski, who not only decried the effects of the welfare state but also referred to New Orleans's poor as "sheep" and "parasites."

Poverty is a matter of culture, not just money.

Most decent people, whatever their politics, will recoil from such dehumanizing rhetoric. But the "culture of poverty" argument itself cannot be so easily dismissed. Yes, some people are poor because of bad luck or catastrophic illness; but chronic, multigenerational poverty is another matter. Yes, poverty in the African-American community results largely from the terrible legacy of a racism that, for generations, denied blacks not only equal opportunity but basic civil rights. But whatever its historical root causes, poverty also perpetuates itself (across racial lines) through a variety of self-defeating habits and behaviors: dropping out of high school, not acquiring marketable job skills, having children without means to support them, even running afoul of the law. In some poor neighborhoods, being a drug dealer is a source of higher status than working in a legitimate job.

The fact that poverty is a matter of culture, not just money, is illustrated by the immigrant experience. Many immigrants start from scratch when they come to the United States, and succeed in rising out of poverty. For them, the American dream is not a myth. Data from the Urban Institute show that while recent immigrants in 1980 and 1990 were twice as likely as native-born Americans to live in poverty, this disparity disappeared for immigrants who had lived in this country for 10 years or more. (In fact, in 2003, according to the Census Bureau, immigrants who were naturalized US citizens had a slightly higher median income than native-born citizens.) This success story includes black immigrants from the Caribbean and Africa, who on average earn substantially more than native-born African-Americans.

Dangerous Ground

To discuss the culture of poverty is to tread on dangerous ground. One can easily come across as patronizing and condescending, as preaching to the poor from one's middle-class perch—or, worse yet, as bashing the poor for their lack of good character. Here, it's important to remember that good cultural habits are usually not a matter of inherent virtue. Most of us, if born into bad circumstances, would have likely ended up trapped in the same self-defeating patterns.

Yes, some people manage to overcome multiple social handicaps and break the cultural habits of their environment. But that takes extraordinary energy, determination, and self-sufficiency. Megan McArdle, an editor at *The Economist*, notes on her weblog, *Asymmetrical Information*, that while conservatives are right in many ways about the causes of poverty, they need to be less moralistic and "a lot more humble."

McArdle also notes that such a diagnosis of the problem leaves us with no ready prescription: Spending more money won't cure poverty, and reforming culture is something that's easier said than done. On the public policy level, we can improve the schools and do something to ease the burden of healthcare costs for men and women in low-paying jobs. But if anyone can change the culture of poverty, it's community activists working in the trenches. And such change is likely to take a long time.

Lack of Support Leads War Veterans into Poverty and Homelessness

Saul Landau

Saul Landau is an author, commentator, and filmmaker on foreign and domestic policy issues as well as a senior fellow at the Institute for Policy Studies.

At an Oakland California freeway exit ramp, a disheveled young man held up a sign: "Help a Gulf War vet." I gave him a dollar. Drivers behind me began to blow their horns, so I didn't ask him if he had fought in Gulf War I or II.

Several days later, getting gas in Hayward, California, I spotted a 'Support our Troops' bumper sticker at the pumps. I worked up the nerve to ask the driver what he had personally done to offer backing to the fighting men and women overseas.

The white, late middle aged, clean shaven, well-dressed individual, wearing a neatly ironed sport shirt, pointed to a smaller sticker on his bumper: Semper Fi.

"I served in the Marine Corps in Vietnam," he sneered. "My loyalty doesn't ebb and flow with the tides of the media," he boasted. "I support the President 100%."

Supporting the troops the Bush way costs nothing.

I told him I didn't mean to be pushy, but how, I asked, did his agreement with [George W.] Bush help people in harms way in Iraq; or when they returned and needed jobs, housing and counseling for post traumatic stress disorders?

Saul Landau, "Support Our Troops: It Costs Nothing," *Mother Jones*, July 25, 2006. www.motherjones.com. Reproduced by permission of Institute for Policy Studies.

"Hmph," he snorted. "You're one of those demonstrating liberal draft dodgers." He assumed a semi-threatening pose, shook his head as if I didn't merit the energy it would take him to throw a punch.

You can have all of the yellow ribbons on cars that say 'Support Our Troops' that you want, "but it's when they take off the uniform and transition back to civilian life that they need support the most," says Linda Boone, executive director of The National Coalition for Homeless Veterans.

Supporting the troops the Bush way costs nothing. Indeed, those who chant loudest in this cause pay less in taxes than previously to support the fighting men and women abroad. Those who want to actually do something for the almost two hundred thousand military men and women in the Afghan and Iraqi messes get scant help from Bush or his Republican Congress.

Lack of Government Support

Homecoming for veterans of war can produce deep distress, rather than a joyful reentry to civilian life. The U.S. government has proven itself prolific at starting wars with little debate about what happens to its soldiers—but not adept at winning them, especially when their opponent fights back. In Korea, Vietnam and Iraq, U.S. troops with superior technology fought hard, but those who started and commanded the wars could not provide a strategy for winning them.

The Veterans Administration admits that hundreds of Iraqi vets already live on the streets.

Worse, the Korean and Vietnam Wars seem to have taught the war-makers little. High tech and well-trained troops do not substitute for knowledge of the enemy's history and reality, without which solid strategy becomes impossible.

Nor do slogans provide for the real needs of veterans who did the dirty work. I remember sitting in university classes next to bitter Korean War vets in the 1950s. They benefited from the GI bill, which paid for their education and helped them buy homes. "Yeah, a great deal," one said to me after we left a history class. "I killed people, saw my buddies killed and wounded. What for?"

So the government would get me through college? Subsequent vets, however, haven't even received GI Bill benefits. Often, loneliness has become their companion in the transition to civilian life. The beggar holding the sign at the off ramp represents one of hundreds of thousands of former warriors who didn't convert easily from war to peace. The Veterans Administration [VA] admits that hundreds of Iraqi vets already live on the streets. The vets suffer from a residual stress from daily insurgent bombs and that makes it tough to adjust to civilian life. Others can't find or hold a job and thus cannot afford to rent a house or apartment.

In March 2002, before Bush stuck the country into the Iraq quagmire, a VA report (VA Programs for Homeless Veterans) stated that "one-third of the adult homeless male population and nearly one-quarter (23%) of all homeless adults have served their country in the armed services."

The VA estimated that "more than 250,000 veterans may be homeless on any given night and that twice as many veterans experience homelessness over the course of a year. Many other veterans are considered at risk because of poverty, lack of support from family and friends and precarious living conditions in overcrowded or substandard housing. Almost all (97 percent) homeless veterans are male and the vast majority are single. About 45 percent of homeless veterans suffer from mental illness and, with considerable overlap, slightly more than 70 percent suffer from alcohol or drug abuse problems."

Add thousands more to this list, those who have recently returned from Iraq. My neighbor, an EMT [emergency medical technician] and acupuncturist specializing in pain relief, joined a Marine medical reserve unit so he could actually "support our troops." He hated the Iraq war, he said, "but those young people out there are our friends and neighbors and need all the support they can get." The Marines have yet to call him to serve even as the death (creeping toward 3,000 in Iraq) and wounded (near 20,000) count mounts. The President has yet to announce a clear plan for U.S. withdrawal [as of July 2006].

Violence escalates and the question on soldiers' minds, "when will we go home?" does not get addressed. The reason for the war "originally weapons of mass destruction and links to terrorism, long dismissed for lack of evidence" remains vague: war on terrorism. That enemy will not surrender, as every GI knows.

On November 17, 2005, former Marine Officer, Congressman John Murtha, reported on the House floor that he had "been visiting our wounded troops in Bethesda and Walter Reed almost every week since the beginning of the war. And what demoralizes them is not the criticism. What demoralizes them is going to war with not enough troops and equipment to make the transition to peace." But the Administration will not raise the issue of a draft, which they assume would cause campus unrest and cohere public opposition as it did in the 1960s and 70s.

The VA is flooded with cases of depression, particularly related to amputations, as well as post traumatic stress disorder, a condition that accompanies war.

Returnees from Iraq witnessed friends losing limbs or dying. They also saw dead and wounded Iraqi women and children after U.S. bombs and shells hit their homes. The troops who massacred Iraqis in Haditha in November 2005 or raped a girl and murdered her family in Tikrit in March 2006 are "two of many examples of aberrant behavior"—[who] lost their balance during the war itself.

Others lose it later. The military budget contains fat and exclusive contracts to Halliburton and other companies to supply troops in Iraq and Afghanistan, but Bush has not made it a budget priority to help them afterwards. The VA is flooded with cases of depression, particularly related to amputations, as well as post traumatic stress disorder, a condition that accompanies war.

In New York City, twenty six year old Herold Noel, a homeless Iraqi war vet, sleeps in his jeep. He parks in places where police will not ticket him. "I saw a baby decapitated when it was run over by a truck—I relived that every night." In Iraq, Noel drove a fuel truck for the military.

"Our troops are cracking under the pressure and pain," wrote Steve Hammons. "Non-stop danger, buddies being blown to bits, urban warfare, ever-present roadside bombs and many other very severe stressors are pushing them over the edge."

Defense Secretary Donald H. Rumsfeld said he is "truly saddened that anyone could have the impression that I or others here are doing anything other than working urgently to see that the lives of the fighting men and women are protected and are cared for in every way humanly possible." Rumsfeld wanted "soldiers, the sailors, the airmen, the Marines to know that we consider them to be America's true treasure, and I thank them and I thank their families."

Treasure? That's what the contracting companies get in Iraq; what Exxon-Mobil has made because war contributes to the rise in oil prices. But Rumsfeld has offered little DOD [Department of Defense] "treasures" for those he allegedly cares for "in every way." He has not supported needed therapy or economic aid for the returning troops.

Next time you see a "Support our Troops" bumper sticker, think about how little the government has done to actually help them and how much it has done to get them killed, wounded and screwed-up for the rest of their lives. [The Bush] Administration ranks high on the list of patriotic rhetoric spouting and at the bottom for actually supporting the troops. Iraqi veterans have come to learn this cruel lesson.

Homelessness Is Caused by Poverty and a Lack of Affordable Housing

National Coalition for the Homeless

The National Coalition for the Homeless is a national network of people committed to ending homelessness.

Two trends are largely responsible for the rise in homelessness over the past 20–25 years: a growing shortage of affordable rental housing and a simultaneous increase in poverty. Below is an overview of current poverty and housing statistics, as well as additional factors contributing to homelessness. . . .

Homelessness and poverty are inextricably linked. Poor people are frequently unable to pay for housing, food, childcare, health care, and education. Difficult choices must be made when limited resources cover only some of these necessities. Often it is housing, which absorbs a high proportion of income that must be dropped. Being poor means being an illness, an accident, or a paycheck away from living on the streets.

In 2005, 13.3% of the U.S. population, or 38,231,521 million people, lived in poverty. Both the poverty rate and the number of poor people have increased in recent years, up from 12.5% or 1.1 million in 2003. 36% of persons living in poverty are children; in fact, the 2004 poverty rate of 17.6% for children under 18 years old is significantly higher than the poverty rate for any other age group.

Two factors help account for increasing poverty: eroding employment opportunities for large segments of the workforce and the declining value and availability of public assistance.

National Coalition for the Homeless, "Why Are People Homeless?" June 2008. www
.nationalhomeless.org. Reproduced by permission.

Eroding Work Opportunities

Media reports of a growing economy and low unemployment mask a number of important reasons why homelessness persists and, in some areas of the country, is worsening. These reasons include stagnant or falling incomes and less secure jobs which offer fewer benefits.

While the last few years [before 2008] have seen growth in real wages at all levels, these increases have not been enough to counteract a long pattern of stagnant and declining wages. Low-wage workers have been particularly hard hit by wage trends and have been left behind as the disparity between rich and poor has mushroomed. To compound the problem, the real value of the minimum wage in 2004 was 26% less than in 1979. Although incomes appear to be rising, this growth is largely due to more hours worked—which in turn can be attributed to welfare reform and the tight labor markets. Factors contributing to wage declines include a steep drop in the number and bargaining power of unionized workers; erosion in the value of the minimum wage; a decline in manufacturing jobs and the corresponding expansion of lower-paying service-sector employment; globalization; and increased nonstandard work, such as temporary and part-time employment.

For many Americans, work provides no escape from poverty.

Declining wages, in turn, have put housing out of reach for many workers: in every state, more than the minimum wage is required to afford a one- or two-bedroom apartment at Fair Market Rent. A recent U.S. Conference of Mayors report stated that in every state more than the minimum-wage is required to afford a one or two-bedroom apartment at 30% of his or her income, which is the federal definition of affordable housing. In 2001, five million rental households had "worst case housing needs," which means that they paid more than half their incomes for rent, living in severely substandard housing, or both. The primary source of income for 80% of these households was earnings from jobs.

The connection between impoverished workers and homelessness can be seen in homeless shelters, many of which house significant numbers of full-time wage earners. In 2007, a survey performed by the U.S. Conference of Mayors found that 17.4% of homeless adults in families were employed while 13% of homeless single adults or unaccompanied youth were employed. A survey of 24 U.S. cities found that 13% of persons in homeless situations are employed. Surveys in past years have yielded the percentage of homeless working to be as high as 26%. In a number of cities not surveyed by the U.S. Conference of Mayors—as well as in many states—the percentage is even higher.

The future of job growth does not appear promising for many workers: a 1998 study estimated that 46% of the jobs with the most growth between 1994 and 2005 pay less than $16,000 a year; these jobs will not lift families out of poverty. Moreover, 74% of these jobs pay below a livable wage ($32,185 for a family of four).

Thus, for many Americans, work provides no escape from poverty. The benefits of economic growth have not been equally distributed; instead, they have been concentrated at the top of income and wealth distributions. A rising tide does not lift all boats, and in the United States today, many boats are struggling to stay afloat.

The Decline in Public Assistance

The declining value and availability of public assistance is another source of increasing poverty and homelessness. Until its repeal in August 1996, the largest cash assistance program for poor families with children was the Aid to Families with Dependent Children (AFDC) program. The Personal Responsibility and Work Opportunity Reconciliation Act of 1996 (the federal welfare reform law) repealed the AFDC program and replaced it with a block grant program called Temporary Assistance to Needy Families (TANF). Current TANF benefits and Food Stamps combined are below the poverty level in every state; in fact, the current maximum TANF benefit for a single mother of two children is 29% of the federal poverty level. Thus, contrary to popular opinion, welfare does not provide relief from poverty.

Welfare caseloads have dropped sharply since the passage and implementation of welfare reform legislation. However, declining welfare rolls simply mean that fewer people are receiving benefits—not that they are employed or doing better financially. Early findings suggest that although more families are moving from welfare to work, many of them are faring poorly due to low wages and inadequate work supports. Only a small fraction of welfare recipients' new jobs pay above-poverty wages; most of the new jobs pay far below the poverty line. These statistics from the Institute for Children and Poverty are particularly revealing:

In the 2001 Institute for Children and Poverty study, 37% of homeless families had their welfare benefits reduced or cut in the last year. More strikingly, in Bucks County and Philadelphia, PA, and Seattle, WA, more than 50% had their benefits reduced or cut.... Among those who lost their benefits, 20% said they became homeless as a direct result. Additionally, a second study of six states found that between 1997 and 1998, 25% of families who had stopped receiving welfare in the last six months doubled-up on housing to save money, and 23% moved because they could not pay rent.

Former welfare families appear to be experiencing homelessness in increasing numbers.

Moreover, extreme poverty is growing more common for children, especially those in female-headed and working families. This increase can be traced directly to the declining number of children lifted above one-half of the poverty line by government cash assistance for the poor.

The Effects of Leaving Welfare

As a result of loss of benefits, low wages, and unstable employment, many families leaving welfare struggle to get medical care, food, and housing. Many lose health insurance, despite continued Medicaid eligibility: a study found that 675,000 people lost health insurance in 1997 as a result of the federal welfare reform legislation, including 400,000 children. Moreover, over 725,000 workers, laid off from their jobs due to the recession in 2000, lost their health insurance. When the economy began recovering in 2003, only about 137,000 of these people regained their coverage. According to the Children's Defense Fund, over nine million children in America have no health insurance, and over 90 percent of them are in working families.

In addition, housing is rarely affordable for families leaving welfare for low wages, yet subsidized housing is so limited that fewer than one in four TANF families nationwide lives in public housing or receives a housing voucher to help them rent a private unit. For most families leaving the rolls, housing subsidies are not an option. In some communities, former welfare families appear to be experiencing homelessness in increasing numbers.

In addition to the reduction in the value and availability of welfare benefits for families, recent policy changes have reduced or eliminated public assistance for poor single individuals. Several states have cut or eliminated General Assistance (GA) benefits for single impoverished people, despite evidence that the availability of GA reduces the prevalence of homelessness.

People with disabilities, too, must struggle to obtain and maintain stable housing. In 2006, on a national average, monthly rent for a one-bedroom apartment rose to $715 per month which is a 113.1% of a person on Supplemental Security Income's (SSI) monthly income (priced out in 2006). In 1999, in more than 125 housing market areas, the cost of a one-bedroom apartment at Fair Market Rent was more than a person's total monthly SSI income. However, in 2006, for the first time, the national average rent for a studio apartment rose above the income of a person who relies only on SSI income. Today, only nine percent of non-institutionalized people receiving SSI receive housing assistance.

Presently, most states have not replaced the old welfare system with an alternative that enables families and individuals to obtain above-poverty employment and to sustain themselves when work is not available or possible.

A Lack of Affordable Housing

A lack of affordable housing and the limited scale of housing assistance programs have contributed to the current housing crisis and to homelessness.

The loss of affordable housing puts even greater numbers of people at risk of homelessness.

The gap between the number of affordable housing units and the number of people needing them has created a housing crisis for poor people. Between 1973 and 1993, 2.2 million low-rent units disappeared from the market. These units were either abandoned, converted into condominiums or expensive apartments, or became unaffordable because of cost increases. Between 1991 and 1995, median rental costs paid by low-income renters rose 21%; at the same time, the number of low-income renters increased. Over these years, despite an improving economy, the affordable housing gap grew by one million. Between 1970 and 1995, the gap between the number of low-income renters and the amount of affordable housing units skyrocketed from a nonexistent gap to a shortage of 4.4 million affordable housing units—the largest shortfall on record. According to HUD [Department of Housing and Urban Development], in recent years the shortages of affordable housing are most severe for units affordable to renters with extremely low incomes. Federal support for low-income housing has fallen 49% from 1980 to 2003.

More recently, the strong economy has caused rents to soar, putting housing out of reach for the poorest Americans. After the 1980s, income growth has never kept pace with rents, and since 2000, the incomes of low-income households has declined as rents continue to rise. The number of housing units that rent for less than $300, adjusted for inflation, declined from 6.8 million in 1996 to 5.5 million in 1998, a 19 percent drop of 1.3 million units. Furthermore, the U.S. Department of Housing and Urban Development defines these Extremely Low Income (ELI) families as ones that earns less than 30% of their region's median family income. In the U.S., ELI households earn about $18,800 annually. Because housing should only consume about 30% of income, these households can afford to spend approximately $470 on rent per month. Less than one in ten renter households actually live in an area where the Fair Market Rent for a studio apartment is in this affordability range for an ELI household. The loss of affordable housing puts even greater numbers of people at risk of homelessness.

The lack of affordable housing has led to high rent burdens (rents which absorb a high proportion of income), overcrowding, and substandard housing. These phenomena, in turn, have not only forced many people to become homeless; they have put a large and growing number of people at risk of becoming homeless. A 2001 Housing and Urban Development (HUD) study found that 4.9 million unassisted, very low-income households—this is 10.9 million people, 3.6 million of whom are children—had "worst case needs" for housing assistance in 1999. Although this figure seems to be a decrease from 1997, it is misleading since, in the same two-year span, "the number of units affordable to extremely low-income renters dropped between 1997 and 1999 at an accelerated rate, and shortages of housing both affordable and available to these renters actually worsened."

Too Little Assistance

Housing assistance can make the difference between stable housing, precarious housing, or no housing at all. However, the demand for assisted housing clearly exceeds the supply: only about one-third of poor renter households receive a housing subsidy from the federal, state, or a local government. The limited level of housing assistance means that most poor families and individuals seeking housing assistance are placed on long waiting lists. From 1996–1998, the time households spent on waiting lists for HUD housing assistance grew dramatically. For the largest public housing authorities, a family's average time on a waiting list rose from 22 to 33 months from 1996 to 1998—a 50% increase. The average waiting period for a Section 8 rental assistance voucher rose from 26 months to 28 months between 1996 and 1998. Today the average wait for Section 8 Vouchers is 35 months.

Only a concerted effort to ensure jobs that pay a living wage, adequate support for those who cannot work, affordable housing, and access to health care will bring an end to homelessness.

Excessive waiting lists for public housing mean that people must remain in shelters or inadequate housing arrangements longer. For instance, in the mid-1990s in New York, families stayed in a shelter an average of five months before moving on to permanent housing. In a survey of 24 cities, people remain homeless an average of seven months, and 87% of cities reported that the length of time people are homeless has increased in recent years. Longer stays in homeless shelters result in less shelter space available for other homeless people, who must find shelter elsewhere or live on the streets. In 2007, it was found that average stay in homeless shelters for households with children was 5.7 months, while this number is only slightly smaller for singles and unaccompanied children at 4.7 months.

A housing trend with a particularly severe impact on homelessness is the loss of single room occupancy (SRO) housing. In the past, SRO housing served to house many poor individuals, including poor persons suffering from mental illness or substance abuse. From 1970 to the mid-1980s, an estimated one million SRO units were demolished. The demolition of SRO housing was most notable in large cities: between 1970–1982, New York City lost 87% of its $200 per month or less SRO stock; Chicago experienced the total elimination of cubicle hotels; and by 1985, Los Angeles had lost more than half of its downtown SRO housing. From 1975 to 1988, San Francisco lost 43% of its stock of low-cost residential hotels; from 1970 to 1986, Portland, Oregon lost 59% of its residential hotels; and from 1971 to 1981 Denver lost 64% of its SRO hotels. Thus the destruction of SRO housing is a major factor in the growth of homelessness in many cities.

Finally, it should be noted that the largest federal housing assistance program is the entitlement to deduct mortgage interest from income for tax purposes. In fact, for every one dollar spent on low income housing programs, the federal treasury loses four dollars to housing-related tax expenditures, 75% of which benefit households in the top fifth of income distribution. In 2003, the federal government spent almost twice as much in housing-related tax expenditures and direct housing assistance for households in the top income quintile than on housing subsidies for the lowest-income households.

Thus, federal housing policy has not responded to the needs of low-income households, while disproportionately benefiting the wealthiest Americans. . . .

Homelessness results from a complex set of circumstances that require people to choose between food, shelter, and other basic needs. Only a concerted effort to ensure jobs that pay a living wage, adequate support for those who cannot work, affordable housing, and access to health care will bring an end to homelessness.

Homophobia Is a Cause of Youth Homelessness

Colby Berger

Colby Berger is director of gay/lesbian/bisexual/transgendered/ queer (GLBTQ) services at The Home for Little Wanderers, a nonprofit child and family service agency in Boston, and a faculty member of The Family Institute of Cambridge, Massachusetts.

By all accounts gay, lesbian, bisexual, and transgendered [GLBT] youths comprise a disproportionate number of at-risk youths across the U.S. They are substantially more likely than are straight youths to experience homelessness, whether because they run away or because they're forced to leave home by their families. They're more likely to attempt suicide and more likely to commit truancy or to drop out of high school altogether to avoid an intolerable situation.

While exact numbers are often hard to come by, studies going back to the 1980's have generally found that between 25 and 40 percent of homeless and runaway youths are GLBT-identified (the numbers vary by region and by methodology [of assessment]). For example, in a fairly recent survey of social service agencies in large U.S. cities, agents in Los Angeles estimated that between 25 and 35 percent of street kids were gay, while those in Seattle pegged the figure at 40 percent. The National Network of Runaway and Youth Services has estimated that 20 to 40 percent of youths who become homeless each year are lesbian, gay, or bisexual. Assuming GLBT youths comprise somewhere between 5 and 10 percent of all young people, all of these estimates indicate that these youths are greatly over-represented in the whole population of at-risk youths.

Colby Berger, "What Becomes of At-Risk Gay Youths?" *The Gay & Lesbian Review Worldwide*, vol. 12, no. 6, November–December 2005, pp. 24–25. Copyright © 2005 *The Gay & Lesbian Review Worldwide*. Reproduced by permission.

It is of course not their sexual orientation per se but instead the homophobia to which they're subjected that makes for an intolerable home situation and paves the path to homelessness. And while being gay is the common denominator of this group of youths, their sexual orientation intersects a number of other factors—race, ethnicity, class, access to resources, and prior system involvement—in determining whether GLBT youths find themselves in a safe and loving home or on the street. Young people who have support from even one adult, whether a teacher, a mentor, or a relative, show significantly greater levels of coping ability and resilience than those who do not.

Sometimes there's outright homophobia in residential programs, including both verbal and physical harassment.

Young people who end up living on the streets have typically experienced homophobia in multiple environments. Having grown up in a family and community that rejected them and destroyed their self-esteem, they're often made to endure homophobia from adults who are meant to provide care. A young person could end up on the streets for any number of reasons; it is common to assume that youngsters who are homeless have been kicked out of their home after coming out, or that they're running away for fear of being the victim of homophobic attacks from family members or at school. While this is the case for some, another segment of youths who are especially at risk are those who become involved with a department of social services or the juvenile justice system as a result of any number of factors—substance abuse (by oneself or by family members), domestic violence, school truancy, being a victim of neglect, the death of a parent, among others—and then slipping through the cracks in the system. In situations where young people are removed from their homes for any of these reasons due to ongoing concern for their well-being, they're usually placed in the child welfare system under the care of a state's department of social services.

A Lack of Services

The general mandate for social workers is to place these youths in the least restrictive and most supportive environment that they can find. Sometimes this means finding a foster family, a group home, or other residential placement. There is typically a dearth of available foster families in the system to begin with, and few are willing to work with young people who have emotional or behavioral problems. Fewer still are interested in fostering GLBT youths, many of whom arrive with emotional and behavioral issues as a result of the homophobia they've endured. Those who are not matched with a family are placed in a residential program, group home, or independent living program. Staff people who work in these environments, like most human service professionals, rarely have training or experience in GLBT issues and are often unprepared to serve the youths in their care. Sometimes there's outright homophobia in residential programs, including both verbal and physical harassment, which can become so unbearable that gay youths feel safer living on the streets than in the home to which they've been assigned.

The lack of safe and supportive services available to GLBT youths is something that governments and service agencies need to address. In Massachusetts, the largest agency serving at-risk youths is the Home for Little Wanderers, where I serve as GLBTQ Training Manager [and at present as director of services]. Founded in 1799, the Home has been one of the most effective child service agencies in the U.S., with a staff of over 700 people working in twenty distinct programs and serving many thousands of children and families every year. The mission of the Home is to ensure the healthy emotional, mental, and social development of children at risk, their families, and their communities. We do this through an integrated system of prevention, advocacy, research, and direct care services. The Home, while a traditional social service agency in some respects, has over time developed a steadfast commitment to providing services specifically tailored to GLBT clients. More recently, the Home has taken the lead in developing an approach to training social service providers who work with this clientele, one that has received national attention.

Specialized Programs

Over the years the Home has developed a number of programs to serve the GLBT population, including Healthy Strong and Proud, Tobacco Education for Gay & Lesbian Youth (TEGLY), Different Directions, and the Waltham House group home. Healthy Strong and Proud, an HIV prevention and education program, and TEGLY's tobacco education program both employ GLBT youths to conduct outreach and provide information to their peers. Different Directions, a component of the Child and Family Counseling Center, provides individual and group outpatient counseling, psychological and neuropsychological testing, and medication evaluation, prescription, and follow-up services for its clients. The Home hired a dedicated director to oversee these programs, to support the internal work with clients throughout the agency, and to develop further services to meet the needs of the GLBT youth in out-of-home care. The newest and perhaps the most groundbreaking of all of its services, Waltham House, is a group home for GLBT youths from age fourteen to eighteen. When it opened, Waltham House was the first residence of its kind in New England and the only group home to exist for this population outside New York and Los Angeles.

Waltham House opened its doors in October of 2002. Despite its nationally unique status, two months later it was serving only four clients and lacked incoming referrals, so we made outreach a priority. We were hearing horrendous stories from the teens in our care about their experiences, often about being bounced from placement to placement within the child welfare system and encountering homophobia from many of the adults charged with their care. Given the research showing that GLBT youths are disproportionately represented in state systems, it was clear that we were not connecting with the enormous number of kids we knew were living in silence. We determined from talking with young people and their social workers that most adults did not have the skills or resources to talk openly with teens about sexual orientation, let alone understand why a gay youth might not be safe in many well-regarded programs.

Specialized Training Needed

In the past, homeless GLBT youths and those "in the system" have often been paired with adults who make placement decisions without the knowledge of this population that would allow them to make appropriate recommendations. Many youths were not even identified as such by case workers. And even when young people felt safe enough to come out to their case worker, the latter often didn't have the resources needed to research the various options to ensure placement in a supportive environment. The Home for Little Wanderers recognized that our practice of educating all of our employees about GLBT issues could be extended to other providers for the benefit of all. We applied for and received funding from the Tides Foundation to develop a training model for use with social workers in Massachusetts. The Department of Social Services was a willing partner in this effort. In the end, the Home's team of trainers educated nearly 2,000 social workers, lawyers, case managers, administrators, policy makers, and family stabilization units about GLBT youth issues.

The training curriculum led participants through a series of interactive exercises on topics such as the power of language and terminology, the connection between identity and behavior, and an analysis of current research findings on GLBT youth. Discussions were conducted about local resources and practical strategies for communicating openly and respectfully with all youths on issues of gender identity and sexual orientation.

It is essential that young people be provided with services that can meet their social, emotional, and physical needs.

As a result of this training and the uniqueness of Waltham House, the Home quickly came to be viewed, both locally and nationally, as a leader in GLBT youth issues. In response to the training initiative, the Home witnessed a dramatic increase in inquiries about providing further training, offering consultation on clients in therapeutic settings, conducting staff development on GLBT issues in schools, and accepting client referrals to Waltham House, along with numerous requests for more information about starting up programs similar to Waltham House. It became evident that in order to meet the demand and fill the training gap that clearly exists, the Home would need to create a full time staff position dedicated to training and consultation on these issues. The position, GLBT Training Manager, now focuses on responding to external requests for training, public speaking, and consultation on both a local and national level.

At Waltham House we sometimes claim that we will have been successful when we put ourselves out of business, which will happen when all residential programs and schools are safe for GLBT youth and programs like Waltham House are no longer needed, Until then, it is essential that young people be provided with services that can meet their social, emotional, and physical needs. Accomplishing this will entail opening more GLBT-centered programming in other states, assisting traditional and mainstream human service agencies to make their programming GLBT-friendly, and, most importantly, educating people about the harmful and pervasive effects of homophobia and the havoc it can wreak on the lives of young people. It is our hope that professionals in all areas of human services will incorporate anti-homophobia and GLBT issues training into their professional development tracks and credentialing. If academic institutions offering degrees in psychology, sociology, education, and criminal justice provided opportunities for students to learn about GLBT identity and development, professionals in these fields would be better prepared to provide safe and supportive services to all of their clients, including one that has all too often been inadequately served in the past.

CHAPTER 3

Do Government Welfare Programs Help the Poor?

Chapter Preface

State and federally funded social welfare programs include a variety of payments and services in the United States, including Medicare and Medicaid, unemployment insurance, food stamps, and direct payments through the Temporary Assistance for Needy Families (TANF) program. While social welfare assumes many forms, the term "welfare" usually refers to the direct assistance given through TANF—prior to 1997 known as Aid to Families with Dependent Children (AFDC). Welfare programs, especially those that involve direct payments, have always been controversial in the United States.

Most social welfare programs did not exist in the United States prior to the Social Security Act, signed by President Franklin D. Roosevelt in 1935 as part of the New Deal. Politicians and commentators continue to argue about whether or not to scale back, or even eliminate, some of the programs. The movement to reduce welfare programs stands in stark contrast to many European countries that have extensive social welfare systems, largely supported by the citizens of those countries. Denmark, for example, provides free education all the way through college, free health care, and a variety of other generous social programs. Countries with extensive welfare programs also usually have higher taxes than countries without such programs; Danes, for instance, pay over 40 percent of their income in taxes. Countries with extensive welfare programs also tend to have less poverty and homelessness than those without. Denmark has one of the lowest unemployment rates in the world and one of the highest levels of income equality among inhabitants; some have claimed that these statistics explain Denmark's ranking as having the happiest people on the planet.

There has been much disagreement in the United States about whether it is a good idea having welfare programs in place to keep people out of poverty or to keep them from being homeless. Critics such as Michael D. Tanner, author of *The Poverty of Welfare*, believe in the total elimination of government welfare programs and call for private solutions to social problems, believing that welfare programs meant to help the poor cause more harm than good. Proponents of welfare programs believe that the higher taxes are worthwhile if they can prevent citizens from falling below a certain level of poverty or from becoming homeless. The opponents of welfare achieved a partial victory in 1996, when President Bill Clinton signed the Personal Responsibility and Work Opportunity Reconciliation Act into law, reforming welfare by moving away from federal cash assistance for the poor. Welfare critics believe that this reform has helped to decrease poverty, whereas many opponents of the reform, such as author and activist Barbara Ehrenreich, believe that the reform was racist, misogynist, and led to more desperation among the poor: "The message is clear: Do not complain or make trouble; accept employment on the bosses' terms or risk homelessness and hunger," Ehrenreich writes. The viewpoints in this chapter debate the value of government welfare programs and welfare reform.

Welfare Reform Has Helped People Out of Poverty

Michael Tanner

Michael Tanner is a senior fellow at the Cato Institute where he heads research on domestic policies. He is the author of The Poverty of Welfare: Helping Others in Civil Society.

On Aug. 22, 1996, President [Bill] Clinton signed the Personal Responsibility and Work Opportunity Reconciliation Act, a bill that despite its obscure title represented the most extensive revision of federal welfare policy in more than 30 years. Among other things, the bill ended the legal entitlement to welfare benefits, established time limits and work requirements for participation in the program, and gave states much more authority to establish other requirements and restrictions.

At the time, most American liberals predicted disaster. As Katha Pollitt wrote in *The New Republic,* "Wages will go down, families will fracture, millions of children will be made more miserable than ever." One frequently cited study predicted that more than a million children would be thrown into poverty. Welfare advocates painted vivid pictures of families sleeping on sidewalks, widespread starvation, and worse. *The New York Times* opined, "The effect on our cities will be devastating." Senator Frank Lautenberg, a Democrat of New Jersey, predicted "hungry and homeless children" would be walking our streets "begging for money, begging for food, even . . . engaging in prostitution." *The Nation* prophesied that "people will die, businesses will close, infant mortality will soar." You would have expected to step over bodies in the streets.

Ten years on, we see that these claims were about as correct as intelligence estimates on Iraq. Welfare rolls are down.

Michael Tanner, "Welfare Reform—What Worked: Ten Years Later, Results Suggest Critics Were Wrong," *San Francisco Chronicle,* August 21, 2006, p. B5. Reproduced by permission of the author.

As [the Department of] Health and Human Services statistics show, roughly 2.5 million families have left the program, a 57 percent decline. Some of this undoubtedly resulted from the growing economy, especially in the late 1990s, but today, welfare rolls remain down despite the post-9/11 economic slowdown.

At the same time, poverty rates remain well below those before welfare reform was enacted. According to the Census Bureau, child poverty rates declined from more than 20 percent in 1996 to 17.8 percent today [2006]. Roughly 1.6 million children were lifted out of poverty. Perhaps even more impressively, since 1996, the poverty rate among black children has fallen at the fastest rate since figures have been recorded. Dependent single mothers, the group most heavily impacted by welfare reform, account heavily for this decline. Since the enactment of welfare reform, the poverty rate for female-headed families with children has fallen from 46 to 28.4 percent—a decline greater than that of any other demographic group.

Former Welfare Recipients Better Off

Most of those who left welfare found work, and of them, the vast majority work full-time. It is true that most of their first jobs were entry-level positions, paying on average $16,000 per year. That's not much, but for many, it's an improvement. As you would expect, studies show that as these former welfare recipients gain work experience, their earnings and benefits increase. And, for better or worse, many continue to receive other forms of government assistance.

It is clear that the critics of welfare reform were wrong.

Surveys of former welfare recipients indicate that they themselves believe their quality of life has improved since leaving welfare, and they are optimistic about their futures.

The Manpower Demonstration Research Corporation reveals that a majority of former welfare recipients believe that their lives will be better in one to five years. Many of these recipients actually praise welfare reform for encouraging them to look for work, for giving them a fresh start, and for giving them a chance to make things better for themselves and their children. Both single mothers and their children appear to benefit psychologically from the dignity of working.

Of course welfare reform has not been perfect. A hardcore group of long-term recipients remains trapped in dependency, and poverty rates remain too high. Out-of-wedlock birthrates, while lower than they were, remain a problem. A few former recipients have fallen through the cracks. But by almost any measure you can think of, it is clear that the critics of welfare reform were wrong.

Yet the same critics raise similar scare stories when reforms to other government programs, from Medicare and Medicaid to Social Security, are discussed. Once again we are hearing that any changes, reductions, or "privatization" of these programs will lead to widespread poverty, suffering and corpses on every corner. Given the critics' record on welfare reform, maybe we should be more skeptical the next time they say the sky is falling.

Some Welfare Programs for the Homeless Are a Good Investment

Philip Mangano

Philip Mangano is executive director of the U.S. Interagency Council on Homelessness, which is responsible for providing federal leadership for activities to assist homeless families and individuals.

When President [George W.] Bush called on the nation to reduce and end chronic homelessness in 2003, few people were optimistic that such a goal was achievable. Many were cynical about the motivation. After all, hadn't the nation focused on this issue long enough to know that change was improbable?

For 25 years, those of us on the front line of the problem were frustrated that nothing seemed to work. People experiencing homelessness were shuffled and cycled from street, to emergency room, to shelter, while we waited for some positive news.

That news arrived when the Department of Housing and Urban Development (HUD) unveiled new research conducted by communities across the country showing that the number of homeless people living on the streets and languishing in shelters is down—dramatically.

According to the data, between 2005 and 2007, the number of people experiencing chronic homelessness—our most vulnerable and disabled neighbors—dropped from nearly 176,000 to fewer than 124,000. That represents a decrease of 52,000 or nearly 30 percent.

What accounts for this documented decrease, the largest in our nation's history? What has moved the nation from being demoralized that street homelessness seemed to be an intractable part of our social landscape, to being re-moralized that change is possible, both visible and quantifiable?

The answer is straightforward. In partnership with the federal government, states and communities are now planning to end homelessness with a new approach. If good intentions, well-meaning programs, and humanitarian gestures could have gotten the job done, homelessness would have been history decades ago.

After years of managing the crisis and experiencing what doesn't work, mayors, governors, and county executives are learning what does. That is evident in more than 500 communities, large and small, from coast-to-coast that are partnered in more than 350 plans to end homelessness in 10 years. These plans are shaped around business principles, daring to couple the verb "end" with the noun "homelessness." That collaboration is complemented by a partnership of 20 federal agencies and a provider community attuned to offering housing.

Economic Thinking Fuels New Approach

Economic thinking is also fueling this new approach. Through nationwide cost studies, cities are learning that people experiencing chronic homelessness are very expensive to the public purse. They are often randomly ricocheting through very expensive health and law enforcement systems—emergency rooms of hospitals, acute addiction and mental health services, police, court, and sometimes incarceration facilities.

Studies show that costs associated with those who are the most vulnerable and disabled range from $35,000 to $150,000 per person annually. Chronically homeless people are "high fliers" in many community systems. In these same communities, the annual cost of the solution, permanent supportive housing, ranges from $13,000 to $25,000 per person. You don't need to be [multibillionaire] Warren Buffett to figure out which is the better investment. Housing is the central antidote, both morally and economically.

Putting business approaches to work for homeless people just makes sense. Discover what works, what is field-tested and evidence-based, and invest old and new resources in those initiatives. When cities and communities do that, they see visible results on their streets and in the lives of homeless people.

The good news is supported by the fact that there are now more resources available than ever before. The Administration and Congress have made record investments for the last seven straight years, and President Bush has proposed an unprecedented eighth consecutive year of increase, more than $5 billion for fiscal 2009.

The outcomes confirm that the chronic homelessness strategy of investing in innovative solutions is working.

We can now talk about these increases as investments and anticipate a return in the lives of homeless people. The rapid dissemination of innovation practiced by the Interagency Council [on Homelessness] assures elected officials that they have equal access to the best ideas, and that their investments are making a difference. Investing in initiatives that have been developed by innovators makes common sense—and dollars sense.

Some of these innovations include Housing First initiatives to move people rapidly into housing to provide stability for the person and cost efficiency for the taxpayer; Street-to-Home engagement strategies to relocate people quickly off the street with the intent of housing; and Project Homeless Connect, a one-day, one-stop strategy to increase access to resources that end homelessness.

President Bush's seemingly improbable marker to end homelessness is being realized across our nation by a nonpartisan partnership that understands that on this issue there are no Democrats or Republicans but simply Americans partnering to end a national disgrace.

There is much more to be done for people who remain homeless, both families and individuals. But the outcomes confirm that the chronic homelessness strategy of investing in innovative solutions is working. That achievement is moving us closer to a tipping point in ending the homelessness of all of our neighbors.

Welfare Reform Has Increased Poverty

Stephen Pimpare

Stephen Pimpare is associate professor of political science at Yeshiva College and Wurzweiler School of Social Work in New York City and the author of A People's History of Poverty in America.

On August 22 [2004] we mark the eighth anniversary of the Personal Responsibility and Work Opportunity Reconciliation Act [PRWORA] welfare reform. Republicans have predictably hailed this landmark as a resounding success, but Democrats, too, have found cause to celebrate: after all, ninety-eight Democratic Representatives and twenty-five Democratic Senators, [2004 presidential candidate] John Kerry among them, helped pass the law, which was then signed, of course, by Democrat Bill Clinton. The next attempt to reauthorize the PRWORA now looms (its seventh temporary extension expires September 30 [2004]), and while Congress will surely consider alterations at the margins, few seem eager to propose fundamental change. They should, for the bipartisan Washington consensus is wrong. Welfare reform has failed.

Welfare Reform Increased Poverty

Yes, welfare rolls have been cut in half (although in many states they are on the rise again), but that is a very narrow measure of success, one which only suggests that reform, as intended, pushed women off the rolls and made it difficult for others to get on.

It is not a measure of reduced need. Quite the contrary: according to the Department of Health and Human Services, by 2000 only half of those poor enough to be eligible for aid received it (about eighty percent did so in the 1980s and early 1990s).

Reform proponents have also made much of the fact that poverty rates fell in the mid-1990s, but there is no evidence to suggest that welfare reform was the cause. Instead, it was more likely the result of modestly higher wages at the lower end of the labor market, thanks to the relatively low unemployment of the recent boom; families working more hours; and the expansion of the Earned Income Tax Credit (which, while a genuine boon to the working poor, is also a government subsidy to employers who pay low wages).

As data from the Economic Policy Institute show, had we not enacted welfare reform poverty would have probably declined further than it did. Welfare reform increased poverty. Regardless, overall poverty rates have been on the rise again, as have child poverty rates, and more of those who are poor are very poor: according to the Children's Defense Fund, by 2001 more African American children were living in deep poverty than at any time since such data have been collected.

Former Welfare Recipients Are Struggling

Meanwhile, in cities large and small homelessness has risen to historic levels, higher even than during the homelessness crisis of the 1980s.

Throughout the nation soup kitchens and food pantries are stretched beyond capacity, struggling and failing to meet new need, much of it from working people whose wages simply haven't kept up. According to the Urban Institute, one-third to one-half of those who left welfare had difficulty providing food for their families. Half or more former recipients are poor (many are poorer than they were before), and some sixty percent of those who left the rolls in 2002 were unemployed. This is success?

What's more, welfare reform has been expensive, despite claims in the Republican Contract with America that reform could save some $40 billion.

According to the GAO [Government Accountability Office], in 1997 alone states received $4.7 billion more than they would have without reform. While some of that new money has been used to fund child care and training programs, many states have used those funds for unrelated expenses. In 2003 and 2004, the Independent Budget Office reports, New York State used more than $1.3 billion in welfare funds to close budget gaps.

Nor have poor women been made less "dependent," another canard; they have instead been made more dependent upon men (as the PRWORA and its marriage incentives intended), or upon the already scarce resources of their friends and neighbors, the caprice of private charity providers, and the vagaries of the low-wage labor market. This too was intended. The US Chamber of Commerce and other business interests, quite active behind the scenes during reform debate, understood the potential rewards: an expanded pool of low-wage workers, and fat new contracts for service provision and administration.

Welfare reform increased poverty.

Public Money in the Private Sector

For-profit and not-for-profit contractors have done quite well. In 2001, state and local governments spent more than $1.5 billion on contracts for basic TANF [Temporary Assistance for Needy Families] services and administration, nearly one-third of which were awarded to private companies; in every state but South Dakota some welfare services were privatized. Accenture (formerly Andersen Consulting, of Enron infamy), Ross Perot's EDS, Citigroup, Lockheed Martin, and others have all gotten a piece of the lucrative new welfare pie. This is not reform, but redistribution, yet another instance of public monies lining private pockets.

This too was anticipated. "Compassionate conservatism" founder Marvin Olasky and other anti-welfare reformers insisted in the early 1990s that to redeem the failed War on Poverty we should emulate the faith-based charity system of the late nineteenth century. We did, by cutting cash relief, requiring work in exchange for aid, and privatizing service provision, just as almost all large American cities did in the Gilded Age.

But Olasky read that history rather selectively, for the nineteenth-century reforms in New York, Baltimore, Philadelphia and elsewhere that he lauded ultimately failed: need among the poor exploded, unrest in the cities grew, and subsidies to private charities grew so large and corrupted that reformers recanted, fought anew to return relief to public control, and then helped expand it, laying the groundwork for the innovations of the Progressive Era and New Deal—the very programs our new breed of reformers seek to undo in a broad effort, it sometimes seems, to return us to the Gilded Age.

Now welfare has dropped off the political radar screen; reauthorization ranked number twenty-two in Project Censored's 2004 list of least-reported stories. There is still time to make up for that failure, but to do so we need the courage of our Gilded Age forebears. We must set aside the shallow conventional wisdom and take a clear-eyed look at what reform has done, and at who has really benefited.

Such an effort would make a fine addition to campaign-season discussion about the appropriate use of public power and public funds, and would be a fitting anniversary gift.

Welfare Programs Make Poverty Worse

David Boaz

David Boaz is executive vice president of the Cato Institute, a libertarian public policy research foundation in Washington, D.C.

Too many journalists seem unable to break free of their old assumptions, even when new evidence should cause some new thinking. Three articles in the Sept. 22 [2005] edition of the *Washington Post* endorsed the view that giving more money to poor people and poor countries can solve the problem of domestic and global poverty. It's remarkable that so many smart people in our society are unaffected by the evidence that such transfer programs just don't work.

Transfer Payments Do Not Work

In a front-page article, two reporters talked about the destitute people fleeing Hurricane Katrina and wondered if America would finally face the problem of poverty. They quoted a foundation president who lamented that Americans "ignore the problems of poverty" until a catastrophe happens. They suggested that only a renewed "War on Poverty" could both help the poor and tell us whether Republicans are ready and able to govern.

A column by David Broder, the dean of Washington journalists, likewise deplored the miserly treatment of the poor. Even [President] Lyndon Johnson, he said, the architect of the War on Poverty, "diverted the resources it required to the other war, in Vietnam."

Meanwhile, a *Post* editorial called for more aid to the governments of poor countries. It suggested that rich countries

David Boaz, "Time for New Thinking about Poverty," Cato Institute, October 10, 2005. www.cato.org. Republished with permission of Cato Institute, conveyed through Copyright Clearance Center, Inc.

measure their commitment to development by a benchmark that emphasizes the amount of aid along with trade, investment, and other criteria.

In every case the assumption that transfer payments are the solution is not even explicitly stated; it's just taken for granted. But where's the evidence supporting this for welfare and foreign aid?

The United States has spent $9 trillion (in current dollars) on welfare programs since President Johnson launched the War on Poverty in 1965. Critics have challenged this figure, saying it includes more than welfare alone. It does include more than Aid to Families with Dependent Children, now known (hopefully) as Temporary Assistance to Needy Families (TANF); it also includes food stamps; Medicaid; the Special Supplemental Food Program for Women, Infants, and Children (WIC); utilities assistance under the Low-Income Home Energy Assistance Program (LIHEAP); housing assistance under a variety of programs, including public housing and Section 8 Rental Assistance; and the free commodities program. Clearly, those are all transfer programs for the poor.

Welfare created a cycle of illegitimacy, fatherlessness, crime, more illegitimacy, and more welfare.

Look at Louisiana alone: Michael Tanner, author of *The Poverty of Welfare*, writes, "The federal government has spent nearly $1.3 billion on cash welfare (TANF) in Louisiana since the start of the [George W.] Bush administration. That doesn't count nearly $3 billion in food stamps. Throw in public housing, Medicaid, Child Care Development Fund, Social Service Block Grant and more than 60 other federal anti-poverty programs, and we've spent well over $10 billion fighting poverty in Louisiana."

Welfare Makes People Dependent

If all that spending didn't cure poverty, then surely more spending isn't the answer. Indeed, maybe it's the problem. Welfare and other aid programs ensnare people, leading them to become dependent on their monthly check rather than finding jobs and starting businesses. In 1960, just before the Great Society's dramatic increases in welfare programs, the out-of-wedlock birth rate in the United States was 5 percent. After 30 years of rising welfare benefits, the rate was 32 percent; young women had come to see the welfare office, not a husband, as the best provider. Welfare created a cycle of illegitimacy, fatherlessness, crime, more illegitimacy, and more welfare.

Welfare is a powerful lure away from the world of work.

Likewise, the United States has spent over $1 trillion on foreign aid. And yet, the [Bill] Clinton administration reported that "despite decades of foreign assistance, most of Africa and parts of Latin America, Asia and the Middle East are economically worse off today than they were 20 years ago." Government-to-government aid has tended to strengthen governments in poor countries at the expense of business and individuals and has made governments increasingly dependent on their rich lenders. Few countries have "graduated" from aid to self-sufficiency. After all that aid, according to a National Bureau of Economic Research study, sub-Saharan Africa is actually poorer than it was 30 years ago.

It's not even that the *Post* reporters weren't aware of the facts. In the 19th paragraph, the front-page story notes that "there are more than 80 poverty-related programs, which in 2003 cost $522 billion." The next line reads, "Yet despite those programs, 37 million Americans continue to live in poverty."

Maybe "despite" is the wrong word. The reporters should consider the possibility that the sentence should read "Because of those programs, 37 million Americans continue to live in poverty."

Similarly, the editorial notes that other policies such as free trade and liberal immigration laws may benefit poor countries more than government-to-government aid. But the editorial writers still can't break free of the idea that giving taxpayers' money to bad governments will help their oppressed citizens.

It's time for new thinking about poor people and poor countries. Transfer payments don't work; they trap both people and countries in a state of dependence instead of self-reliance.

Markets work. People who get a job—any job—and stick with it until they find a better one will stay out of the welfare-and-poverty trap. But welfare is a powerful lure away from the world of work.

Markets work internationally, too. If you rate all the countries in the world by the degree of economic freedom they have, that turns out also to be a ranking of their prosperity. Per capita income in the freest 20 percent of countries is 10 times what it is in the least free countries. Those latter countries need property rights, free markets, honest courts, and low taxes—not foreign aid.

And reporters need new glasses, to let them see the evidence in front of them rather than relying on their outmoded assumptions.

Welfare Programs for the Homeless Exacerbate the Problem

John Derbyshire

John Derbyshire is an author and columnist who writes on culture, politics, race, history, immigration, and other topics.

I had an interesting week recently visiting Colorado and points west to promote my new book. Met a lot of great people, saw some places I'd never seen before, had a lot of fun with math fans and NR/NRO [*National Review* and *National Review Online*] readers, got home safely to Mrs. Derb and the little ones. (Also to hundreds of unread e-mails. I am sorry if you e-mailed me during that time. I'm doing my best.) My trip included Berkeley and downtown San Francisco. The bookstore events in these places went fine, and many thanks to all who showed up. It's not the events I want to comment on, though. It's the street people.

The Homeless in San Francisco

Berkeley was pretty bad, but I had sort of expected that, having spent time in Ann Arbor [Michigan, in 2002]. University towns tend to have a lot of street people, for reasons that don't take much figuring out. It was downtown San Francisco that really surprised me. I wanted to go look at the new Asian Arts Museum, which is in the old municipal library building, on one side of the city's main downtown plaza. Nearby is a spiffy *new* library, which cost $137[million] and was the subject of some scathing comments by [American author] Nicholson Baker.

So there I was in downtown San Francisco, right after a very successful book-signing event at Stacey's on Market Street,

John Derbyshire, "End of the Line," *National Review Online*, May 19, 2003. www .nationalreview.com. Reproduced by permission.

making my way between these grand heroic buildings under the bright California sun. It wasn't the afterglow of promotional success, or the magnificence of the buildings, or the sunlight and the wonderful, warm California air that I was noticing, though. What was mostly presenting itself to my eyes, ears, and nose were the street people—platoons, companies, *battalions* of them. I have never seen so many street people. Here a ragged, emaciated woman mumbling to herself and making complicated hand gestures like a Buddhist priest; there a huge black-bearded Rasputin of a man in a floor-length heavy overcoat, pushing a shopping cart piled high with filthy bundles; across the way a little knot of florid winos arguing loudly and ferociously about something; sitting on the sidewalk where I passed, a youngish black woman, gaunt and nearly bald, with some sort of skin disease all over her face and scalp, croaking something at me I couldn't understand.

Half the lunatics, drunks, and drug addicts in America—in the *world*, I wouldn't be surprised—are right here in the center of their city.

A homeless adult [in San Francisco] on county welfare gets $395 a month, more than in any neighboring jurisdiction.

Welfare for the Homeless

Why? This is a great puzzle to the city's irredeemably liberal Board of Supervisors and their soul mates in the local press. One of the latter, Ilene Lelchuk of the *San Francisco Chronicle*, recently began a sentence thus: "With San Francisco's homeless population growing despite the millions of dollars the city spends annually to help its most desperate residents . . ." Note that word "despite." *We spend more and more on the homeless, and still their numbers increase. How can this be?* What a strange and wonderful thing is the liberal mind! (Recall the similarly clueless *New York Times* headline, though this one I am quoting from memory: "Prison Population Swells Despite Falling Crime Levels.")

San Francisco is indeed generous to street people. A homeless adult on county welfare gets $395 a month, more than in any neighboring jurisdiction. There is no requirement that recipients have any roots in the county, nor is there any work requirement. I am willing to bet, though I haven't found a source, that there is not even a requirement for U.S. citizenship. So far as I have been able to discover, there are no requirements whatsoever. You just quit your job, move to a place with the most agreeable climate in the world, cease attending to matters of personal hygiene, get yourself a substance habit, and sign on for a hundred bucks a week, no questions asked. And Ms. Lelchuk wonders why the "homeless" population is growing!

I suppose the citizens of San Francisco have gotten used to the situation by slow degrees, but for a visitor arriving in the downtown area from some more civilized place—in my case, Denver—the spectacle is very shocking. The street people leer at you, yell at you, sometimes harass you. If you are a woman, they make lewd remarks at you. Near the entrance to the Asian Art Museum (which, by the way, is lovely, with a $10 admission fee to keep out undesirables—unlike the new library opposite, which, I am told, has been totally colonized), they are as dense as shoppers in a street market, and you have to pick your way carefully through them. Acts of violence are common—a young man was shot dead in Market Street a few days ago, a block or two from the tony bookstore where I had done my book signing. Stabbings are frequent.

And of course, the street people stink. Even in the open spaces downtown, you can't avoid the stink. It is probably worse than it used to be before the U.N. [United Nations] Plaza fountain was fenced off in March, as the street people had been taking baths in the fountain. They had also been urinating, defecating, and discarding drug paraphernalia there—the last to such a degree that the water was dangerous with chemical contaminants, even if you could bring yourself to ignore the waste products. The city used to do a daily clean-up, but at last they got fed up and erected a chain-link fence round the whole thing in the teeth of, it goes without saying, vehement protests from "advocates for the homeless."

This United States of America was founded on the notion of self-support.

By [2002] the larger situation had already got so bad that city voters were presented with a November ballot initiative, Proposition N, under whose terms that $395 monthly cash handout to the winos would be reduced to $59, the balance being replaced by city-provided food and shelter. This "Care not Cash" initiative was passed, with 60 percent of voters in favor of it. That, of course, outraged the city's lefty activists, who immediately challenged the vote in court. On May 8 Superior Court Judge Ronald Quidachay ruled that only the Board of Supervisors can set city welfare policy, and that the ballot initiative was therefore invalid. The hundred-dollars-a-week handouts to anyone that shows up will continue—in a city that is looking at a $350[million] deficit [in 2003].

Dealing with the Homeless

When you cross the United States from the east coast, San Francisco is the end of the line, the last stop on the long cross-country trail. It is also the end point of liberalism, as foreseen by Rudyard Kipling: the point at which "all men are paid for existing and no man must pay for his sins." You can't go any further than this geographically without falling into the ocean; you can't go any further than San Francisco has gone in yielding to the "rights" of people who acknowledge no balancing duties, no responsibility whatsoever to their fellow citizens, nor even to their own persons.

This United States of America was founded on the notion of self-support, of people taking care of their families, joining with neighbors to solve common problems in a humane and sensible way. Those common problems would include the occasional citizen, like Huckleberry Finn's pap, who could not, or stubbornly would not, look after himself, and for whom some public provision should be made. When a person "came upon the town," the town would give him some minimal aid, while of course private citizens, if they felt inclined, could exercise the virtue of private charity to any degree they wished. The recipient was, however, expected to defer to community standards. If he persistently committed gross violations of those standards, he was locked up or institutionalized. This was a sound system, widely admired outside our borders. Listen to the most American of American presidents, Calvin Coolidge.

"The principle of service is not to be confused with a weak and impractical sentimentalism."

"Self-government means self support."

"The normal must care for themselves."

"I have no respect for anybody who cannot take care of himself."

It would be very easy to deal with the "homeless problem": enact, or reenact, vagrancy laws, sweep the bums, junkies, and lunatics off the streets, incarcerate them in well-supervised but Spartan facilities until they showed some inclination to cease being a nuisance, an embarrassment and a danger to their fellow citizens. Those facilities should be open to the press. Perhaps they should even be open to the general public, since apparently 40 percent of San Franciscans enjoy the company of stinking winos.

But that, of course, would never do. The "homeless" have "rights" that must be respected—the right to crap in public fountains, for instance, the right to shoot themselves up with deadly drugs in public squares, the right to shriek gibberish at passers-by, and the right to expose themselves to female office workers heading for the subway station. If we didn't respect those rights—why, we wouldn't be America, would we?

CHAPTER 4

What Strategies Would Benefit the Poor and the Homeless?

Chapter Preface

Poverty and homelessness exist worldwide, and experts engage in an ongoing debate about the severity of the problem. One of the difficulties of developing a consistent standard for measuring poverty is the vast disparity between the impoverished in the developed world and the impoverished in the developing world. The poor in the United States or other developed nations might have housing and possess consumer items such as cars, while many of the poor in the developing world must do without adequate shelter, food, and clothing, and they cannot even hope to have access to cars or televisions. The World Bank estimates that 1.4 billion people, one quarter of the population of the developing world, live in poverty. Regardless of where the poor live, whether in the United States or worldwide, policy makers have struggled with the questions of what should, and could, be done about it.

One strategy for easing global poverty is to give money to charities that work to eliminate poverty. Peter Singer, a professor of philosophy at Princeton University, believes strongly that people living above the poverty line in the developed world should do something about global poverty; he asserts that there is a moral imperative to give at least 1 percent of one's annual salary to initiatives that aim to combat global poverty. Singer maintains that although "we tend to think of charity as something that is 'morally optional'—good to do, but not wrong to fail to do," he believes that "those who do not meet even the minimal 1% standard should be seen as doing something that is morally wrong." For Singer, withholding money from someone who may die without help—when that money is not needed by the giver to survive—is the moral equivalent of walking by a drowning child in a shallow pond and not doing anything to help.

Many argue, however, that giving handouts is not the way to fight poverty of any kind. Far from being a morally good thing to do, the *Wall Street Journal* claims that "to offer mere handouts, however well-intentioned, is to discount the innate capacity of those on the receiving end and, ultimately, to devalue their worth." Giving handouts to people risks disrespecting and insulting them. The correct solution, according to Adam Meyerson of the Philanthropy Roundtable, is "giving the poor the means to create wealth for themselves."

The debate over how best to address the problem of poverty reveals the complexity of the issue and the difficulty of finding a solution to a problem that endures worldwide. The viewpoints in this chapter debate these issues.

A Variety of Approaches Are Needed to Cut Poverty

The Center for American Progress

The Center for American Progress is a think tank dedicated to improving the lives of Americans through ideas and action.

Thirty-seven million Americans live below the official poverty line. Millions more struggle each month to pay for basic necessities, or run out of savings when they lose their jobs or face health emergencies. Poverty imposes enormous costs on society. The lost potential of children raised in poor households, the lower productivity and earnings of poor adults, the poor health, increased crime, and broken neighborhoods all hurt our nation. Persistent childhood poverty is estimated to cost our nation $500 billion each year, or about four percent of the nation's gross domestic product. In a world of increasing global competition, we cannot afford to squander these human resources.

The Center for American Progress [in 2006] convened a diverse group of national experts and leaders to examine the causes and consequences of poverty in America and make recommendations for national action. In this report, our Task Force on Poverty calls for a national goal of cutting poverty in half in the next 10 years and proposes a strategy to reach the goal.

Poverty in America

Our nation has seen periods of dramatic poverty reduction at times when near-full employment was combined with sound federal and state policies, motivated individual initiative, supportive civic involvement, and sustained national commit-

The Center for American Progress, "From Poverty to Prosperity: A National Strategy to Cut Poverty in Half," April 25, 2007. This material was created by the Center for American Progress. www.americanprogress.org. Reproduced by permission.

ment. In the last six years, however, our nation has moved in the opposite direction. The number of poor Americans has grown by five million, while inequality has reached historic high levels.

Consider the following facts:

- One in eight Americans now lives in poverty. A family of four is considered poor if the family's income is below $19,971—a bar far below what most people believe a family needs to get by. Still, using this measure, 12.6 percent of all Americans were poor in 2005, and more than 90 million people (31 percent of all Americans) had incomes below 200 percent of federal poverty thresholds.

- Millions of Americans will spend at least one year in poverty at some point in their lives. One third of all Americans will experience poverty within a 13-year period. In that period, one in 10 Americans are poor for most of the time, and one in 20 are poor for 10 or more years.

Inequality has reached record highs. The richest 1 percent of Americans in 2005 held the largest share of the nation's income (19 percent) since 1929.

- Poverty in the United States is far higher than in many other developed nations. At the turn of the 21st century, the United States ranked 24th among 25 countries when measuring the share of the population below 50 percent of median income.

- Inequality has reached record highs. The richest 1 percent of Americans in 2005 held the largest share of the nation's income (19 percent) since 1929. At the same time, the poorest 20 percent of Americans held only 3.4 percent of the nation's income.

It does not have to be this way. Our nation need not tolerate persistent poverty alongside great wealth.

A Strategy to End Poverty

The United States should set a national goal of cutting poverty in half over the next 10 years. A strategy to cut poverty in half should be guided by four principles:

- *Promote Decent Work.* People should work and work should pay enough to ensure that workers and their families can avoid poverty, meet basic needs, and save for the future.

- *Provide Opportunity for All.* Children should grow up in conditions that maximize their opportunities for success; adults should have opportunities throughout their lives to connect to work, get more education, live in a good neighborhood, and move up in the workforce.

- *Ensure Economic Security.* Americans should not fall into poverty when they cannot work or work is unavailable, unstable, or pays so little that they cannot make ends meet.

- *Help People Build Wealth.* All Americans should have the opportunity to build assets that allow them to weather periods of flux and volatility, and to have the resources that may be essential to advancement and upward mobility.

We recommend 12 key steps to cut poverty in half:

- *Raise and index the minimum wage to half the average hourly wage.* At $5.15, the federal minimum wage is at its lowest level in real terms since 1956. The federal minimum wage was once 50 percent of the average wage but is now 30 percent of that wage. Congress should restore the minimum wage to 50 percent of the average wage, about $8.40 an hour in 2006. Doing so would help nearly 5 million poor workers and nearly 10 million other low-income workers.

- *Expand the Earned Income Tax Credit [EITC] and Child Tax Credit.* As an earnings supplement for low-income working families, the EITC raises incomes and helps families build assets. The Child Tax Credit provides a tax credit of up to $1,000 per child, but provides no help to the poorest families. We recommend tripling the EITC for childless workers and expanding help to larger working families. We recommend making the Child Tax Credit available to all low- and moderate-income families. Doing so would move as many as 5 million people out of poverty.

- *Promote unionization by enacting the Employee Free Choice Act.* The Employee Free Choice Act would require employers to recognize a union after a majority of workers signs cards authorizing union representation and establish stronger penalties for violation of employee rights. The increased union representation made possible by the Act would lead to better jobs and less poverty for American workers.

- *Guarantee child care assistance to low-income families and promote early education for all.* We propose that the federal and state governments guarantee child care help to families with incomes below about $40,000 a year, with expanded tax help to higher-earning families. At the same time, states should be encouraged to improve the quality of early education and broaden access for all children. Our child care expansion would raise employment among low-income parents and help nearly 3 million parents and children escape poverty.

- *Create 2 million new "opportunity" housing vouchers, and promote equitable development in and around cen-*

tral cities. Nearly 8 million Americans live in neighborhoods of concentrated poverty where at least 40 percent of residents are poor. Our nation should seek to
end concentrated poverty and economic segregation,
and promote regional equity and inner-city revitaliza-
tion. We propose that over the next 10 years the federal
government fund 2 million new "opportunity vouchers"
designed to help people live in opportunity-rich areas.
Any new affordable housing should be in communities
with employment opportunities and high-quality public
services, or in gentrifying communities. These housing
policies should be part of a broader effort to pursue
equitable development strategies in regional and local
planning efforts, including efforts to improve schools,
create affordable housing, assure physical security, and
enhance neighborhood amenities.

- *Connect disadvantaged and disconnected youth with
  school and work.* About 1.7 million poor youth aged 16
  to 24 were out of school and out of work in 2005. We
  recommend that the federal government restore Youth
  Opportunity Grants to help the most disadvantaged
  communities and expand funding for effective and
  promising youth programs—with the goal of reaching
  600,000 poor disadvantaged youth through these efforts. We propose a new Upward Pathway program to
  offer low-income youth opportunities to participate in
  service and training in fields that are in high-demand
  and provide needed public services.

- *Simplify and expand Pell Grants and make higher education accessible to residents of each state.* Low-income
  youth are much less likely to attend college than their
  higher income peers, even among those of comparable
  abilities. Pell Grants play a crucial role for lower-
  income students. We propose to simplify the Pell grant

application process, gradually raise Pell Grants to reach 70 percent of the average costs of attending a four-year public institution, and encourage institutions to do more to raise student completion rates. As the federal government does its part, states should develop strategies to make postsecondary education affordable for all residents, following promising models already underway in a number of states.

- *Help former prisoners find stable employment and reintegrate into their communities.* The United States has the highest incarceration rate in the world. We urge all states to develop comprehensive reentry services aimed at reintegrating former prisoners into their communities with full-time, consistent employment.

- *Ensure equity for low-wage workers in the Unemployment Insurance system.* Only about 35 percent of the unemployed, and a smaller share of unemployed low-wage workers, receive unemployment insurance benefits. We recommend that states (with federal help) reform "monetary eligibility" rules that screen out low-wage workers, broaden eligibility for part-time workers and workers who have lost employment as a result of compelling family circumstances, and allow unemployed workers to use periods of unemployment as a time to upgrade their skills and qualifications.

- *Modernize means-tested benefits programs to develop a coordinated system that helps workers and families.* A well-functioning safety net should help people get into or return to work and ensure a decent level of living for those who cannot work or are temporarily between jobs. Our current system fails to do so. We recommend that governments at all levels simplify and improve benefits access for working families and improve services to individuals with disabilities. The Food Stamp

Program should be strengthened to improve benefits, eligibility, and access. And the Temporary Assistance for Needy Families Program should be reformed to shift its focus from cutting caseloads to helping needy families find sustainable employment.

- *Reduce the high costs of being poor and increase access to financial services.* Despite having less income, lower-income families often pay more than middle and high-income families for the same consumer products. We recommend that the federal and state governments address the foreclosure crisis through expanded mortgage assistance programs and by new federal legislation to curb unscrupulous practices. And we propose that the federal government establish a $50 million Financial Fairness Innovation Fund to support state efforts to broaden access to mainstream goods and financial services in predominantly low-income communities.

- *Expand and simplify the Saver's Credit to encourage saving for education, homeownership, and retirement.* For many families, saving for purposes such as education, a home, or a small business is key to making economic progress. We propose that the federal "Saver's Credit" be reformed to make it fully refundable. This Credit should also be broadened to apply to other appropriate savings vehicles intended to foster asset accumulation, with consideration given to including individual development accounts, children's saving accounts, and college savings plans.

Cost and Effect

Our recommendations would cut poverty in half. The Urban Institute, which modeled the implementation of one set of our recommendations, estimates that four of our steps would reduce poverty by 26 percent, bringing us more than halfway toward our goal. Among their findings:

- Taken together, our minimum wage, EITC, child credit, and child care recommendations would reduce poverty by 26 percent. This would mean 9.4 million fewer people in poverty and a national poverty rate of 9.1 percent—the lowest in recorded U.S. history.

- The racial poverty gap would be narrowed: White poverty would fall from 8.7 percent to 7 percent. Poverty among African Americans would fall from 21.4 percent to 15.6 percent. Hispanic poverty would fall from 21.4 percent to 12.9 percent and poverty for all others would fall from 12.7 percent to 10.3 percent.

- Child poverty and extreme poverty would both fall: Child poverty would drop by 41 percent. The number of people in extreme poverty would fall by 2.4 million.

- Millions of low- and moderate-income families would benefit. Almost half of the benefits of our proposal would help low- and moderate-income families.

That these recommendations would reduce poverty by more than one quarter is powerful evidence that a 50 percent reduction can be reached within a decade.

Across the nation, there is a yearning for a shared national commitment to build a better, fairer, more prosperous country, with opportunity for all.

The combined cost of our principal recommendations is in the range of $90 billion a year—a significant cost but one that could be readily funded through a fairer tax system. An additional $90 billion in annual spending would represent about 0.8 percent of the nation's gross domestic product, which is a fraction of the money spent on tax changes that benefited primarily the wealthy in recent years. Consider that:

- The current annual costs of the tax cuts enacted by Congress in 2001 and 2003 are in the range of $400 billion a year.

- In 2008 alone the value of the tax cuts to households with incomes exceeding $200,000 a year is projected to be $100 billion.

Our recommendations could be fully paid for simply by bringing better balance to the federal tax system and recouping part of what has been lost by the excessive tax cuts of recent years. We recognize that serious action has serious costs, but the challenge before the nation is not that we cannot afford to act; rather, it is that we must decide to act.

In 2009, we will have a new president and a new Congress. Across the nation, there is a yearning for a shared national commitment to build a better, fairer, more prosperous country, with opportunity for all. In communities across the nation, policymakers, business people, people of faith, and concerned citizens are coming together. Our commitment to the common good compels us to move forward.

Redefining the Poverty Level Would Help Ease the Problem of Poverty

Douglas W. Nelson

Douglas W. Nelson is president and CEO of the Annie E. Casey Foundation, a private charitable organization that works to foster public policies that meet the needs of vulnerable children and families.

The Annie E. Casey Foundation's passionate commitment to helping those children and families who are most vulnerable is matched only by our determination to be guided by quality data and useful indicators. This is illustrated by our KIDS COUNT project and our numerous investments aimed at measuring the impact of our grants on the status, conditions and well-being of the families our grantees are seeking to help. In our judgment, good measures of kid and family conditions are indispensable to good policy decisions and public accountability.

Every year since 1990, we have released an annual *KIDS COUNT Data Book,* which uses the best available data to measure the educational, social, economic and physical well-being of children, state by state. The Foundation also funds a national network of state-level KIDS COUNT projects that provide a more detailed, county-by-county picture of the condition of children. We care about this data because it helps leaders and citizens make better decisions about how to improve the lives of children and their families.

Let me give you an example of what I mean. Several years ago, our KIDS COUNT grantee in Rhode Island developed an

Douglas W. Nelson, "Testimony Before the Subcommittee on Income Security and Family Support of the House Committee on Ways and Means," July 17, 2008. Reproduced by permission.

improved measurement of childhood lead poisoning that was much easier for the public to track and understand. Rhode Island KIDS COUNT's baseline data showed that one in four children in Rhode Island had a history of lead poisoning upon entering kindergarten, and that one in three children in the state's five core cities entered kindergarten with a history of lead poisoning.

The publication of this data sounded an alarm in Rhode Island that this was a serious issue in need of immediate attention. Community leaders responded in many effective ways, including better enforcement of lead laws and enhanced parent education. Their efforts resulted in the development of city and state lead poisoning prevention plans and the passage of a comprehensive lead poisoning prevention law by the General Assembly. The incidence of childhood lead poisoning has decreased significantly during the decade since the indicator was first published—down to 6 percent statewide and 10 percent in the core cities.

The lack of an accurate, credible, and relevant poverty measure has itself become a major impediment to combating poverty effectively.

The Current Poverty Definition

Since its inception nearly 20 years ago, KIDS COUNT has tracked a core set of indices for measuring child need and the effectiveness of programs designed to meet those needs. But, clearly, of all the measures we rely on, none is more fundamental or consequential than how we assess a family's economic standing. That's why Casey has been so distressed at the nation's continued reliance on an outdated, incomplete, and misleading measure of poverty.

All of this is to explain why I am here today and why I believe it is essential that we act now to change our deeply flawed poverty measure. It is essential for a simple reason: the lack of an accurate, credible, and relevant poverty measure has itself become a major impediment to combating poverty effectively. If we want to solve the poverty challenge, step one is to get our heads around the true scope, dimension, and dynamics of the problem.

Today, almost no one would argue that the current poverty definition—which sets the poverty threshold at $21,200 for a family of two adults and two children—yields anything remotely close to a well thought out, accurate measure of who is genuinely poor. Indeed, scholar Nicholas Eberstadt of the American Enterprise Institute has dubbed the poverty measure "America's worst statistical indicator."

The current formula produces a "poverty line" income that may amount to less than 60 percent of what it actually costs a family to meet its basic needs.

Most Americans have a pretty solid sense of what it means for a family to be poor. As Rebecca Blank of the Brookings Institution has said, poor families are folks who do not have enough resources to afford decent housing, to find and hold a job, to be well fed and reasonably healthy and to pay for the things that their children need to be safe and succeed in school. Unfortunately, our current poverty measure—crafted in the 1960s—simply does not reflect this common sense understanding of what it means to be poor in 2008.

The Flaws of Current Indicators

The current measure is flawed in two fundamental ways. First of all, it underestimates the actual cost of paying for the core of basic and routine needs that American families are expected to meet. Developed when food represented one-third of a typical family's budget, the poverty line was drawn by the federal government by calculating the cost of a basic grocery budget and multiplying by three. The dollar figure developed in 1963 has only been adjusted for inflation, even though food is now one-seventh of a typical family's budget, and even though the formula does not take into account the actual cost of other core expenses, such as housing and work-related costs, that take up a much greater portion of family budgets today than they did 40 years ago. In the opinion of some analysts, the current formula produces a "poverty line" income that may amount to less than 60 percent of what it actually costs a family to meet its basic needs.

Ninety percent of the families who end up losing their kids to foster care are poor.

The second basic flaw of the current measure is that it significantly underestimates the total income, resources or benefits that many of today's families actually receive and use to meet those basic needs. The current poverty formula fails to include valuable non-cash benefits such as housing assistance, the Earned Income Tax Credit [EITC], the Child Tax Credit and food stamps. Consequently, the official federal poverty data not only understate the cash and benefits many low-income families enjoy, but also give us no indication of how well some of our key public investments in the economic well-being of low-income families are paying off.

Across the country, children's advocates are rallying around a proposed campaign to cut the nation's child poverty rate in half over the next decade. Yet many of our most promising approaches to improving the economic fortunes of children—expanding the earned-income and child tax credits for working families, extending child care subsidies, increasing the utilization rates for food stamps and other means-tested programs—would never be recognized by today's poverty measure. These are, however, among the very resources and benefits that have the potential to pull families out of the deep and persistent poverty that hurts kids most.

The evidence is overwhelming that when families are entrapped in persistent poverty, childhood problems multiply. Ninety percent of the families who end up losing their kids to foster care are poor. Poor kids are five times more likely to miss learning proficiency benchmarks than kids from families with greater economic security. Kids growing up in poor families are far more likely to drop out of school, get pregnant, or get in trouble with the law. There is every reason to worry that the persistent, sustained poverty that triggers these problems could grow, particularly as more entry level jobs in the American economy are lost to the global labor market. As a result, more families are settling for wages that cannot produce enough to sustain a family at an "American" standard of living.

Persistent structural poverty is a serious drag on American competitiveness, optimism, cohesion and influence in the world. Economists now estimate that child poverty costs the nation about $500 billion a year. That burden will worsen in time. This nation—a dramatically aging one—cannot afford to have as much as a fifth of its children grow up without the skills, supports, connections and opportunities needed to participate in the nation's new economy.

An Accurate Poverty Measure

Unfortunately, the poverty measure as it exists today does not tell us enough about what is actually helping these children. There is ample evidence that the poverty threshold would be higher, and would convey a far more accurate sense of real need, if the poverty measurement objectively reflected how much a family needs to "get by" or "make ends meet" in America today.

Under a number of approaches used in recent years to calculate this "getting by" threshold, a basic family budget would include food, housing, out-of-pocket medical costs, child care, transportation and taxes. Although there were significant regional differences, most of the methods used resulted in a "poverty" standard that was approximately twice the current poverty level. The Economic Policy Institute, for example, which calculated this basic family budget for more than 400 communities, came up with a median budget of $39,984 for a family of four. By contrast, the poverty threshold at the time of the study was just $19,157.

A large part of our work at the Annie E. Casey Foundation focuses on what we call Family Economic Success—the ability of families to secure adequate incomes, stabilize their finances, accumulate savings and live in safe, economically viable communities. In order to determine whether federal policies, and the work of our grantees, are effective, we need a more accurate and relevant measure of how families are progressing financially. At the very least, the measure should be designed to assess whether struggling families have the minimum resources they need to lead safe and healthy lives.

An accurate poverty measure might lead to changes in some of the strategies we use to help families in need. By including food stamps, the EITC, the child tax credit and housing assistance in the poverty measurement, we would be able to better determine who was taking advantage of these programs and who wasn't—and how these families were doing as a result. We might find, for instance, that those who were receiving certain types of government assistance showed greater success at moving out of poverty, while those who weren't remained stuck in place year after year.

Having an accurate poverty measure would also provide us with better information for considering long term, as well as short term strategies—what we call a "two-generation approach" to fighting poverty. Such an approach supports, stabilizes, and empowers low-income working parents through work support programs, while at the same time aggressively equipping their kids with the skills, experiences and values to increase their odds of avoiding hardship, forming intact families and contributing to national prosperity.

Universal preschool and quality child care and after school programs, for example, are considered key tools for ensuring that the next generation of kids is better equipped to move out of poverty. A new approach to calculating poverty could provide a measure of the short and long term success of such strategies and create public and political will to expand those programs that have proven successful in reducing poverty. It could also help re-target programs that are not working as well.

Disagreement About the Measure

Clearly, there are many excellent reasons for changing the poverty measure. Why then hasn't it happened? Why do we tolerate such an egregiously flawed indicator of such a critically important measure of the social and economic status of our nation's citizens—especially when we know how to do better?

There are doubtless lots of reasons. Inertia, convenience, and the advantages of keeping a measure that allows 40 years of longitudinal comparisons all reinforce acceptance of the status quo.

Perhaps even more important, there are real philosophical and political differences about who should be counted as poor. Some critics have consistently preferred changes in the measure that would reduce the numbers of Americans counted as poor. They point to the failure of the current measure to take into account the value of public benefits, and they argue that many who are now counted as poor have far greater access to comforts and conveniences (e.g., cars, televisions, air conditioning) than those counted as poor 40 years ago.

Other critics have favored changes that would increase the number of Americans described as poor. They contend that the amount of money required to minimally support a family—at today's housing, transportation, child care, utility, and medical costs—significantly exceeds the current poverty threshold, and that millions of families with pre-tax incomes well above the official poverty line experience great difficulty in paying for what are now considered the basic requirements of a stable family life.

These two competing perspectives—each harboring some solid, if partial, correctness—have been allowed to paralyze the nation's poverty measurement reform efforts for decades. It's time that we recast the debate beyond an either/or choice to a new common sense consensus that draws thoughtfully from the analyses of both perspectives.

Like any good poverty measure, this new approach would follow data over time in order to understand trends and ensure that policy aimed at fighting poverty is really working.

Changing the Measure

Changing the poverty measurement would also likely result in shifts in the allocation of certain federal funding for some groups. In her 2008 paper, "How to Improve Poverty Measurement in the United States," Rebecca Blank notes that the alternative poverty measurement guidelines developed by the National Academy of Sciences (NAS) resulted in fewer people with large in-kind benefits being classified as poor, an increase in working poor after work expenses were calculated, and changes in the number of elderly poor due to such factors as the subtraction of out-of-pocket medical expenses.

Some dissatisfaction is inevitable among competing groups likely to feel that their interests will be adversely affected by the new numbers. The process, however, will be far less painful if from the beginning the poverty measurement is taken out of the political realm.

For the NAS guidelines or similar approaches to succeed, the Executive Office of the President should no longer have direct control of the poverty measurement. Unlike the vast majority of economic statistics, which are the responsibility of federal statistical agencies, updating the poverty measure is overseen by the Office of Management and Budget. That means any changes in the measure must pass through the White House. Ms. Blank got to the heart of the matter in her recent paper: "If we need an example of why economic statistics should be in the hands of statistical agencies, the long-term stalemate over poverty measurement provides an excellent one!"

At Annie E. Casey, we endorse Ms. Blank's suggestion for assigning to a federal statistical agency the authority to develop an alternative measure of poverty that embraces the key elements of the National Academy of Sciences' approach. That means including non-cash benefits and refundable credits, accounting for child care costs and out-of-pocket medical expenses and, if feasible, adjusting for some regional differences in the cost of living.

Like any good poverty measure, this new approach would follow data over time in order to understand trends and ensure that policy aimed at fighting poverty is really working. I believe that changing the poverty measure should be viewed as part of overall efforts in this country to hold ourselves and our policy makers accountable for honestly confronting the problems faced by those in need—and coming up with clear and measurable responses.

Raising the Minimum Wage Is Necessary to Combat Poverty

Holly Sklar and Paul Sherry

Holly Sklar directs the Business for a Fair Minimum Wage project of Business for Shared Prosperity and is the author of Raise the Floor: Wages and Policies That Work for All of Us. *Paul Sherry is a minister and former president of the United Church of Christ who also coordinates the Let Justice Roll Living Wage Campaign.*

Wages are a bedrock moral issue. Wages reflect our personal values and our nation's values. Wages reflect whether we believe workers are just another cost of business—like rent, electricity or raw materials—or human beings with inherent dignity, human rights and basic needs such as food, shelter and health care.

The minimum wage is where society draws the line: This low and no lower.

Our bottom line is this: A job should keep you out of poverty, not keep you in it.

The federal minimum wage was enacted through the Fair Labor Standards Act of 1938, which also set standards for overtime pay and restrictions on child labor. The Fair Labor Standards Act was designed to eliminate "labor conditions detrimental to the maintenance of the minimum standard of living necessary for health, efficiency and general well-being of workers."

The federal minimum wage has been stuck at $5.15 an hour since September 1997. That's more than eight years [as of 2005] at $5.15 as the cost of living rises. [In 2008 the wage was raised to $6.55 and will be raised again in 2009 to $7.25]. Set too low, the minimum wage is doing the opposite of what the Fair Labor Standards Act intended. It is reinforcing "labor conditions detrimental to the maintenance of the minimum standard of living necessary for health, efficiency and general well-being of workers."

Today's minimum wage is not a fair wage—economically or ethically. It is not good for workers, business or our nation's future.

The American Dream Reversed

The $5.15 minimum wage is lower in value than the minimum wage of 1950—which would be worth more than $6 now, adjusting for inflation. The minimum wage buys less today than it did when Wal-Mart founder Sam Walton opened his first Walton's 5 and 10 in Bentonville, Arkansas in 1951.

Most people remember the 1963 March on Washington for Jobs and Freedom as the occasion where the Rev. Dr. Martin Luther King Jr. gave his famous "I Have a Dream" address. A key demand of the march was "a national minimum wage act that will give all Americans a decent standard of living." The 1963 minimum wage is worth more than $8 in today's dollars.

The real minimum wage—the wage adjusted for inflation—reached its highest point in 1968. It would take more than $9 to match the minimum wage peak of 1968, adjusting for inflation.

The year 1968 is so long ago that most Americans living today were not even born yet. The costs of housing, health care and higher education have all risen dramatically since then. College tuition (public or private), for example, costs more than twice what it did in 1968, adjusting for inflation. But the minimum wage has 43 percent less buying power than it had in 1968—and that buying power keeps shrinking as the minimum wage goes without a raise.

The cost of health insurance has risen so much that family coverage now costs more than the entire annual income of a full-time worker at minimum wage.

- In 1991, family health coverage cost one-fourth of the yearly income of a minimum wage worker.

- In 1998, it took about half the yearly minimum wage.

- By 2005, family health coverage cost $10,880, and a full-time minimum wage was just $10,712.

The typical worker paid minimum wage is an adult, not a teenager living with parents.

Dr. Martin Luther King did not dream that in the year 2005 the minimum wage would not have the buying power of 1950. He did not dream that in this new millennium we would be debating whether to "raise" the minimum wage to the level employers paid in the 1960s.

We are living the American Dream in reverse.

Work Ethic Goes Unnoticed by Paychecks

Contrary to stereotype, the typical worker paid minimum wage is an adult, not a teenager living with parents. Most have high school degrees or more.

Think of women working in garment sweatshops and chain stores.

Think of farmworkers, fast food workers and cannery workers who depend on food banks to help feed their families.

Think of janitors and housekeepers cleaning the homes, offices and hotel rooms of people who make more in a day than they make in a year.

Think of security guards without economic security.

Think of child care workers who don't make enough to make ends meet, much less save for their own children's education.

Think of health care aides taking care of our parents or grandparents—without health benefits, paid sick days or paid vacation.

Think of workers in New York going without heat and health care to keep food on the table.

Think of caregivers in California struggling to care for their own families.

Think of workers in New Orleans with no car or money to escape a hurricane.

Hurricane Katrina [in 2005] exposed depths of poverty and inequality many Americans were shocked to see, and many people around the world were shocked to see in America. If the cataclysm is to bring lasting positive change, it won't be found in windfall profits for politically connected corporations. It won't be found in the rollback of already inadequate labor, environmental, and health and safety standards.

One key to healthy change will be this simple recognition: To protect lives we must shore up the livelihoods upon which people depend everyday—and not just in emergencies. Raising the minimum wage is an urgent priority—and a moral one.

As *Congressional Quarterly* observed: "In the Lower Ninth Ward and other impoverished neighborhoods of New Orleans, people have long waged battle to make ends meet. . . . That was a nearly unattainable goal in a city where many of the jobs were in hotels and restaurants that paid around the federal minimum wage of $5.15 an hour."

Moreover, "widespread poverty also prompted many poor New Orleans families to absorb relatives, creating large, extended families under one roof. This phenomenon actually disguised the number of people unable to support themselves and created a class of what demographers call 'hidden homeless.'" Yet compared to many other places, New Orleans "was not a particularly expensive place to live." Nor was it the most impoverished.

The Wage Ethic

Although one out of four people in New Orleans lived below the official poverty line before Hurricanes Katrina and Rita, New Orleans didn't make the top ten of cities ranked by people living in poverty (with a population of 250,000 or greater). It was tied with Cleveland for 12th place, behind cities as varied as Baltimore, Memphis, Philadelphia, Buffalo, Milwaukee, Long Beach (CA), Atlanta, Newark, Miami, El Paso and Detroit, ranked No. 1 with one out of three people below the poverty line.

No one should be trapped in poverty by low wages. It's time to stop keeping hardworking Americans down and raise the minimum wage.

Polls show that Americans strongly back a higher minimum wage. Most people know that a $5.15 minimum wage—$10,712 a year—just doesn't add up. A single parent with one child would need to work more than two full-time minimum wage jobs to make ends meet. It takes more than three jobs at minimum wage to support a family of four.

Millions of workers find themselves with paychecks above the minimum, but not above the poverty line.

It is time for a just minimum wage, not a minimum wage that just doesn't add up. We need a wage ethic to go with our work ethic.

The Working Poor

The minimum wage has become a poverty wage instead of an anti-poverty wage. This has ripple effects through our workforce and society far beyond minimum wage workers and their families.

The minimum wage sets the wage floor. As the wage floor has dropped below poverty levels, millions of workers find themselves with paychecks above the minimum, but not above the poverty line. Millions of workers are working hard, but can't make ends meet.

As *Business Week* observed in a 2004 cover story on the growing ranks of the working poor, "More than 28 million people, about a quarter of the workforce between the ages of 18 and 64, earn less than $9.04 an hour, which translates into a full-time salary of $18,800 a year—the income that marks the federal poverty line for a family of four."

We have gone so far backwards that one out of four workers makes the $9-and-change-equivalent of the minimum wage of 1968. This includes nearly one out of three women workers, one out of three black workers and more than one out of three Latino workers.

Poverty rates are higher now than in the 1970s thanks in part to the falling minimum wage. Nearly one in three children living below the official poverty line lived in families where someone worked full time year round in 2003—an increase of 75 percent since 1991.

On average, households need about twice the level of the official poverty line to meet basic expenses.

Cycle of Poverty Wages

If poor Americans were a nation, the population would top Louisiana, Mississippi, Alabama, Georgia, Arkansas, Iowa, Kansas, Nebraska, New Hampshire, New Mexico, West Virginia and Washington, DC combined. And that's using the Census Bureau's poverty count of 37 million Americans for 2004, which is based on poverty thresholds that are increasingly outdated and unrealistic.

Millions more Americans can't afford adequate health care, housing, utilities, child care, food, transportation and other basic expenses above the official poverty thresholds. Here are some of the official poverty thresholds for 2004:

- $9,827 for a person under 65

- $9,060 for a person 65 and older

- $13,020 for an adult and child

- $15,205 for two adults and one child

- $19,157 for two adults and two children.

Nationally, on average, households need about twice the level of the official poverty line to meet basic expenses (including minimally adequate housing, utilities, health care, food, child care, transportation, clothing and other personal and household necessities, and taxes—factoring in tax credits such as the Earned Income Credit and Child Tax Credit). The $5.15 minimum wage—$10,712 a year full time—is inadequate for even a single person, much less a family.

According to the Economic Policy Institute's Basic Family Budget Calculator, the national median basic needs budget (including taxes and tax credits) for a one-parent, one-child family was $27,948 in 2004. (Half are below the median, half are above.) Looking at more than 400 U.S. communities, budgets for a one-parent, one-child family ranged from $19,536 in rural Nebraska to $49,848 in Boston, which has the nation's highest housing costs. The national median for a two-parent, two-child family was $39,984; budgets ranged from $31,080 in rural Nebraska to $64,656 in Boston. . . .

The official poverty thresholds are far too low for low-cost rural Nebraska, much less as national yardsticks. The Census Bureau reports that 91 million people—nearly one out of three Americans—were below twice the official poverty line.

Paychecks You Cannot Live On

Around the country, minimum wage earners and other low-paid workers have turned increasingly to food banks and homeless shelters, which cannot keep up with the rising demand. In its 2004 *Hunger and Homelessness Survey*, the U.S. Conference of Mayors found:

- Requests for emergency food increased an average of 14 percent during the past year and 20 percent of the requests went unmet.

- Requests for shelter increased 6 percent and 23 percent of the requests went unmet.

- Among the homeless, 17 percent were employed, as were 34 percent of adults requesting emergency food assistance.

"Poverty and hunger are rapidly becoming a workplace issue," says John Challenger, chief executive officer (CEO) of the employment consulting firm Challenger, Gray & Christmas, which finds more working families living at or below the poverty line. "It should be a very large concern for employers, if for no other reason than the fact that an employee who is worried about where his or her next meal will come from is not going to be very productive."

Past minimum wage increases reduced hunger and food insecurity. Researchers found that "even after controlling for the link between the 1990s economic expansion and food security, the October 1996 and September 1997 increases in the federal minimum wage raised food security and reduced hunger."

The U.S. Conference of Mayors adopted a resolution in 2005, calling for an increase in the minimum wage to "better enable minimum wage job holders to support themselves and their families." The mayors also observed that "the minimum wage is one factor in wide income disparities, as minorities work disproportionately in minimum wage jobs."

In the words of the National Urban League, raising the minimum wage "provides long overdue economic relief for millions of low-wage workers. It is also one important strategy towards closing the poverty gap that threatens American ideals of fairness and equality."

If the "minimum wage" doesn't cover necessities, it's not a minimum wage—it's a minus wage. No matter what job you have, you shouldn't have to choose between eating or heating, child care or health care. . . .

On a Shaky Foundation

The minimum wage is not just about fair pay for workers. It is an essential part of the foundation of our economy and society. We can't have a strong economy built on a widening gap between top and bottom any more than we can have a strong apartment building with an ever more luxurious penthouse at the top and a sinking foundation below. Further weakening that foundation—the direction we are headed—will make things much worse, not better.

The low road, with its low minimum wage, is fiscally, socially and environmentally irresponsible, and morally bankrupt.

Eileen Appelbaum and Annette Bernhardt, co-editors of *Low-Wage America: How Employers are Reshaping Opportunity in the Workplace*, emphasize the importance of the minimum wage in reinforcing advancement for workers, businesses and the economy: "A low wage floor creates incentives for employers to take the easy way out and cut wages to enhance profits. But a higher wage floor . . . pushes firms to invest in new technology, modern management practices, better training and better ways of delivering services in order to raise productivity and profits."

Instead of knocking down the real value of the minimum wage at home and stimulating downward mobility, the United States should be raising the floor here and internationally. It should be advocating for trade rules to advance livable wages around the world instead of setting a bad example at home and encouraging companies like Wal-Mart to drive down wages globally. Everyone has the right to a fair day's pay for a fair day's work whether in the United States, Mexico, South Africa, South Korea, Egypt, Vietnam, China, India or anywhere else. That means dividing revenues more fairly among owners, investors, executives and workers instead of accelerating profits and increased polarization between top and bottom. (In the 2005 ranking of Forbes Global 2000 leading companies in the world—with 66 million employees—total sales rose 13 percent while profits jumped a much-higher 71 percent.)

The low road, with its low minimum wage, is fiscally, socially and environmentally irresponsible, and morally bankrupt. We have to change course. The high road is an economic and ethical imperative.

Education Is an Important Part of a Strategy to Combat Poverty

Jared Bernstein

Jared Bernstein is director of the Living Standards Program at the Economic Policy Institute and the author of All Together Now: Common Sense for a Fair Economy.

Economists may disagree a lot on policy, but we all agree on the "education premium"—the earnings boost associated with more education. But what role can education play in a realistic antipoverty policy agenda? And what are the limits of that role?

First, it depends on whether you're talking about children or adults, and schooling versus job training. And second, the extent to which education is rewarded depends on what else is going on in the economy. . . .

Investment in early childhood has immense benefits. And at the other end of the schooling spectrum, college graduates' wage advantage over those with only a high-school diploma went up dramatically in the 1980s and early '90s. But the premium that high-school graduates enjoy over dropouts has been flat for decades. In 1973, high-school grads earned about 15.7 percent more per hour than dropouts, 15.9 percent in 1989, 16.1 percent in 2000, and 15.5 percent [in 2006]. And for adult workers, the historical record for job-training programs is pretty dismal, though more recent initiatives—with their focus on more carefully targeting training for local labor markets—show much more promise.

Jared Bernstein, "Is Education the Cure for Poverty?" *The American Prospect*, vol. 18, no. 5, May 2007, pp. A17–A20. Copyright © 2007 The American Prospect, Inc. All rights reserved. Reproduced with permission from *The American Prospect*, 11 Beacon Street, Suite 1120, Boston, MA 02108.

Nobody doubts that a better-educated workforce is more likely to enjoy higher earnings. But education by itself is a necessary but insufficient antipoverty tool. Yes, poor people absolutely need more education and skill training, but they also need an economic context wherein they can realize the economic returns from their improved human capital. Over the past few decades, the set of institutions and norms that historically maintained the link between skills and incomes have been diminished, particularly for non-college-educated workers. Restoring their strength and status is essential if we want the poor to reap the benefits they deserve from educational advancement.

Education alone is much less successful in raising employment and earnings prospects than education combined with a strategy of focused job training.

What Research Shows

Julie Strawn of the Center for Law and Social Policy, reviewing an extensive sample of basic education and training programs, concluded that education alone is much less successful in raising employment and earnings prospects than education combined with a strategy of focused job training (with an eye on local demand), "soft skills," and holding out for quality jobs.

One study found that a year of schooling raised the earnings of welfare recipients by 7 percent, the conventional labor economics finding. But given that many of these workers entered the job market in the $6- to $8-an-hour range back in the 1990s, you're talking about moving families closer to the poverty line, not pushing them significantly above it.

Strawn reports that when education is combined with multidimensional job training, readiness, and a quality job search, the returns more than double. One Portland, Oregon, program resulted in a 2.5 percent increase in earnings, a 21 percent increase in employment, and a 22 percent reduction of time spent on welfare (all compared with a control group that didn't get the services).

Education and Training

This finding makes intuitive sense: Programs that combine general education with training specific to both the individual and his or her local labor market work better than ones that fail to combine these activities. (They're also more expensive, but you get what you pay for.) Yet to get to the hub of the strengths and limits of education and poverty reduction, we need to go back to first principles and think about how they interact with the realities of the political economy.

Education is only a partial cure for poverty because of all the other recent changes in the labor market. At least half of the inequality increase has taken place within groups of comparably educated people, and since 2000 that proportion has been increasing. Income-inequality data show that the concentration of income in 2005 is the highest it has been since 1929. Yet research that Lawrence Mishel and I conducted shows that since the late 1990s, the college wage premium has been flat. In real terms, college wages were up less than 2 percent from 2000 to 2006. Even among the highly educated, only some are getting ahead, and lots aren't.

In short, we are not living in a meritocracy, where we can reliably count on people being fairly rewarded for their improved skills. So we need additional mechanisms in place to nudge the invisible hand toward outcomes that are more meritocratic and just.

Skill Demands for the Working Poor

Education is a supply-side policy; it improves the quality of workers, not the quality or the quantity of jobs. A danger of overreliance on education in the poverty debate is that skilled workers end up all dressed up with nowhere nice to go.

Some economists contend that faster rates of technological advance require ever more highly skilled workers, and that demand shifts lead to low wages for the low skilled. But our work at the Economic Policy Institute suggests that while technological changes have always been an important factor in the labor market, the rate of change now is no greater than in the recent past. Technological change is one of the reasons we've doubled the share of college grads but continued to see their unemployment rates in the 2 percent range—we produce and absorb a lot of college grads.

Our economy, however, is still very much structured to produce lots of low-wage jobs. In fact, according to the occupational projections by the Bureau of Labor Statistics, the low-wage sector of our economy will be the source of much job growth over the next decade. The American economy will continue to employ significant numbers of retail salespersons, waiters and waitresses, food-prep workers, home health aides, maids and housekeepers, etc. Of the 30 occupations adding the most jobs to our economy, those requiring the least training make up half of the total.

Demand—the extent of overall growth, how taut the labor market is—matters, as does the extent and nature of inequality, as does the quality of jobs.

Quality of Jobs

The question, thus, is not whether jobs for those with only high-school degrees or even some college will exist or be plentiful in our future (they almost certainly will be); the question is whether the quality of these jobs will help reduce or reinforce working poverty.

In our most recent version of "The State of Working America," we borrow a technique from economists Sheldon Danziger and Peter Gottschalk for analyzing the roles played by multiple determinants of poverty. Their method parses out the roles of race, family structure, economic growth, and inequality, and we add the role of education. . . .

Family poverty rates did not fall much between 1969 and 2000, because major factors were offsetting one another. Improved education lowered family poverty by almost 4 percentage points, a considerable effect. But economic growth and inequality had considerably larger effects. Growth in the overall economy lowered poverty rates by 5.7 points, while inequality raised it by 5.1 points. Family structure added 3 points to family poverty rates over these years, and race added 1 point.

Decompositions of this type are far from definitive; they tend to hold one factor constant and see how things change, then do the same for another factor, etc. But in this case, the results are demonstrative of the main point regarding education in the poverty debate: It's an important part of the story, but it's not the whole story, or even the most important part.

The Education Plus Approach

Demand—the extent of overall growth, how taut the labor market is—matters, as does the extent and nature of inequality, as does the quality of jobs. In the late 1990s, poverty fell to historic lows for those with the lowest education levels, including African Americans and single mothers. Did skills rain from the heavens? Did employers suddenly shed their advanced-skill requirements? Of course not. It was good old-fashioned full employment forcing employers to bid wages up to get—and keep—the workers they needed. And yes, this interacted with welfare reform and a significant expansion of work supports, like the Earned Income Tax Credit, subsidized health and child care, and the minimum-wage increase.

In fact, one could be forgiven for thinking that, except for some of the punitive aspects of welfare reform, we briefly got poverty reduction right during the late 1990s. The one-two punch of full employment and expanded work supports worked to meet the expanding labor supply with even faster growing labor demand, and the subsidies helped to close part of the gap between what people earned and what they needed.

Helping the poor receive more education is part of the answer.

But notice how all of this is unwinding in the 2000s. Unemployment is low, but other indicators—such as labor-force participation and real wage trends—suggest we're not yet at full employment; there's been no expansion of work supports, and even some retrenchment of supports such as the State Children's Health Insurance Program and child care, policies clearly associated with helping the working poor get ahead. The outcome has been predictable and depressing, especially in contrast to the progress we made in the 1990s.

And if education is one key antipoverty strategy, then programs demanding that beneficiaries "work first" often sacrifice the promise of increased returns to education and training on the altar of take-any-job. This approach is not only stingy; it's also shortsighted, as it threatens to diminish the likelihood that those who want to "play by the rules" will realize their economic potential.

Helping the poor receive more education is part of the answer. Whatever their skill level, workers need a context wherein they can be rewarded for their skills, where the benefits of the growth they help to create flow freely their way. This means having a set of protections, institutions, regulations, and social norms in place to keep the greedy fingers of inequality from picking the pockets of the working poor.

Providing Housing Is the Key to Ending Homelessness

Sam Tsemberis, interviewed by Meghann Farnsworth

Sam Tsemberis is the founder of Pathways to Housing, a nonprofit organization that works with homeless people. Meghann Farnsworth is an editorial intern at Mother Jones *magazine.*

In the article "Life on the Inside," in the [January/February 2005] issue of *Mother Jones*, Douglas McGray writes that even when the United States economy was booming and jobs were abundant in the 1990's, millions of people were homeless at some point during a year. The chronically homeless were racking up hundreds of thousands of dollars in emergency care, putting a huge strain on the health care and emergency shelter systems. In addition, millions of federal dollars were being spent on the problem with little to no success. Faced with these staggering numbers, Sam Tsemberis decided that a change in approach was well past due.

After working on various programs with limited success, Tsemberis began to realize that the homeless were not the problem; homelessness was. He stopped assuming he knew what was best for people and started listening. What he heard was not revolutionary or surprising, but it has changed the way homelessness is approached.

In 1992, Tsemberis founded Pathways to Housing on the principle that the chronically homeless need housing first. With a place of their own, Tsemberis felt, the homeless would be in a position to turn the rest of their lives around; with a safe place to sleep and live, other problems such as drug abuse, alcoholism and mental illnesses could be dealt with. With a

Meghann Farnsworth interviews Sam Tsemberis, "Give Me a Home," *Mother Jones*, December 20, 2004. www.motherjones.com. Reproduced by permission.

dedicated team of psychiatrists, nurses and staff, Pathways is delivering the figures to confirm the promise of their approach.

Sam Tsemberis recently spoke with *MotherJones.com* from his home in New York City.

MotherJones.com: Talk about some of the programs you were involved with before starting Pathways to Housing. What was their purpose?

Sam Tsemberis: They were called "outreach programs," and their purpose was to engage people who were mentally ill and not living anywhere. One of the reasons the program was started was that there were so many people out there who appeared not to be able to take care of themselves because of their mental illness. There was a concern that they were a risk both to themselves and to others; we have people here who have psychotic symptoms and they're in public places; it's a precarious situation.

One of the programs consisted of a team that was made up of a social worker, a psychologist, a nurse and a psychiatrist. We would drive around the city, essentially conducting these sidewalk house calls to people who appeared to be in a very precarious state, whose survival was really in question. One of the events that launched the program was the woman who froze to death in New York [1982]. She wasn't the only one who was homeless, mentally ill and died, but she was a case that came to a lot of people's attention. The program was designed to prevent that sort of thing from ever happening again. No one should ever have to die on the streets.

Now, there were actually very few dramatic cases like that. But there were hundreds and hundreds of people we saw who were mentally ill and were living on the streets; we wanted to be able to do something for them. That's where we really began this frustrating process of figuring out where we could refer people. We were trying to get them into housing programs, but there was a huge wall because the housing

were on fixed incomes, like the people who are mentally ill and are on SSI [Supplemental Security Income] are still at the five-, six-hundred dollar income a month level. The market has passed them by. They are not able to compete successfully for the little affordable housing that is around. And once they are on the street, whatever conditions had existed previously are exacerbated because of struggles and traumas of street life.

But there is also this extra component of people with disabilities and people who are poor. I think it is a deeply engrained, cultural belief that if you are somehow poor that you have squandered what was given to you. Or somehow you don't deserve anything. You had a chance and somehow blew it. This is especially true if there is drug use involved. People don't see addiction as an illness, but rather as a voluntary kind of recreational drug use gone awry. So there is a very punitive and moralistic societal value we have about people who are homeless and in desperate need.

There is a program here in San Francisco called Care Not Cash. Part of the funding for the program goes to supportive housing and part gives homeless people money. Do you think just giving money to homeless people is a good way of dealing with homelessness?

It's a wonderful thing to do. It gives them a little control over their lives. Who are we to know what they want and what their priorities are? I found out for sure that the whole clinical, mental health and substance abuse treatment system didn't have a clue about how to prioritize people's needs. The only reason our program is successful is because we let people choose what they want. It wasn't our idea to give them housing first; it was their idea. We just said, "Tell us what you want and we will give it to you."

And suddenly when you do that, you realize all of these people who say, "Oh, these people can't be engaged, they're too psychotic," is not at all true. People who are homeless are listening up and are very eager to vote with their feet. They go right into those apartments. So, I say, give people control of their lives. How can you keep people so completely dependent they can't even make a decision about how to spend 500 bucks, and then, at the same time, expect that they are going to be independent, fully functioning citizens in society? Where are they going to learn those skills, if you have them completely handcuffed?

Who are your clients? Where do they come from?

Over the years, the program has changed really from working with people on the street to working with a lot of people who were homeless and were arrested. There was whole big effort to improve the quality of life on the streets of New York and a lot of other cities too. A lot of people ended up in jail. And so now, instead of going to jail for jumping the turnstile of the subway, you can come into the program if you are mentally ill and homeless. So, some of the places where we are getting our referrals have changed, but essentially the people are the same. They've just been shifted around to different locations as a result of whatever social policy that is flying at the time. The usual way it goes is people immediately want the apartment and a very short time after that they are looking for something to do. Not treatment, really, but a little work, making a little extra money. They want to fix up their place; they want to hold onto it. Having a home is a great motivator.

Once you lose your house you can't hear back from an interview; it's a downward slide very quickly.

There was an article in the Los Angeles Times *in November 2004 that talked about how the city was completely unprepared to deal with the rising number of homeless, including a rising number of families with young kids. Would you say that most cities are unprepared?*

Oh, completely overwhelmed. The numbers are overwhelming.

Why so many families?

It's poverty! You can't really pay the rent with a minimum-wage job. Minimum wage has not kept up at all with the cost of living. People are making six and seven dollars an hour where just to be able to afford a place you have to be making 12 or 15. So a lot of the people who are working at the minimum-wage jobs, even with two jobs, have a hard time paying the rent, especially if there are kids involved—they need a bigger place. It's all about poverty, in a way. Once you lose your house you can't hear back from an interview; it's a downward slide very quickly.

Criminalizing Homelessness Is Ineffective and Violates Rights

National Coalition for the Homeless and National Law Center on Homelessness & Poverty

The National Coalition for the Homeless and the National Law Center on Homelessness & Poverty work to protect the rights of the homeless.

For the past 25 years, cities have increasingly implemented laws and policies that target homeless persons living in public spaces. This trend began with cities passing laws making it illegal to sleep in public spaces or conducting "sweeps" of areas where homeless people were living. In many cities, more neutral laws, such as open container or loitering laws, have been selectively enforced for years. Other measures that cities have pursued over the past couple decades include anti-panhandling laws, laws regulating sitting on the sidewalk, and numerous other measures.

In some cities where a variety of "status" ordinances have resulted in large numbers of arrests, "habitual offenders" are given longer jail terms and classified as criminals in shelters and other service agencies because of their records.

Unfortunately, over the years, cities have increasingly pursued these measures and expanded their strategies to target homeless people, using vague "disorderly conduct" citations to discourage homeless people from moving freely in public. [Recently], cities have increasingly focused on restrictions to panhandling and public feedings. These restrictions only create additional barriers for people trying to move beyond homelessness and poverty.

National Coalition for the Homeless and National Law Center on Homelessness & Poverty, "A Dream Denied: The Criminalization of Homelessness in U.S. Cities," January 2006, pp. 14–18. Reproduced by permission.

Restrictions on Panhandling

Some cities have turned their attention to restricting panhandling in the downtown areas of their cities. These targeted restrictions also often include prohibitions on panhandling near ATMs, bus stops, or outdoor restaurants.

In August 2005, Atlanta passed a fairly comprehensive ban on panhandling in the "tourist triangle" and anywhere in the city after sunset. The ordinance, entitled, "Commercial Solicitation," also bans panhandling within 15 feet of an ATM, bus stop, taxi stand, pay phone, public toilet, or train station in all parts of the city. Upon conviction for a third offense of the ordinance, a violator can be fined up to $1000 or imprisoned for up to 30 days.

Cleveland also passed an anti-panhandling law in July 2005 that, among other things, prohibits panhandling within 20 feet of an ATM, bus stop, or sidewalk café. The law on "aggressive solicitation" also prohibits panhandling within 10 feet of an entrance to a restaurant or parking lot.

Pittsburgh city leaders amended its panhandling ordinance in November 2005. The new bill expands on the existing panhandling ordinance by restricting solicitation for charity to daylight hours. The bill also bans panhandling within 25 feet of an outdoor eating establishment, 25 feet of an admission line, 25 feet of the entrance to a place of religious assembly, within 25 feet of money dispensing areas, and 10 feet of a food vendor or bus stop. The bill also outlaws "aggressive panhandling" and solicitation of money that hinders traffic.

Another trend among cities trying to regulate panhandling includes requiring panhandlers to obtain a license to panhandle. Dayton, for example, prohibits persons from panhandling without a "registration" issued by the Chief of Police. Additionally, in Cincinnati, panhandling without a permit is considered "improper solicitation."

The Minneapolis Chief of Police tried to promote the licensing of panhandlers in May 2005. Service providers and advocates spoke out against the proposed scheme, noting that deeper issues must be addressed instead of criminalizing poor and homeless people. The effort by the Chief of Police has been put on hold, as the Mayor of Minneapolis opposes licensing panhandlers. The Mayor is seeking alternatives to licensing to address panhandling, but has not revealed what those alternatives would be.

Yet another form of targeting panhandlers has emerged in city efforts to encourage people to give to organizations or charities instead of to panhandlers. Baltimore; Nashville; Athens, Georgia; and Spokane all have such campaigns to discourage people from giving to panhandlers.

Restrictions on Feedings

Cities have been further targeting homeless persons by penalizing those offering outdoor feedings for homeless individuals. These city restrictions are frequently aimed at preventing providers from serving food in parks and other public spaces.

In Dallas, beginning in September 2005, a new ordinance penalizes charities, churches, and other organizations that serve food to the needy outside of designated areas of the city. Anyone who violates this ordinance can be fined up to $2000.

In June 2005, Miami also considered passing a law that would prohibit groups from feeding homeless persons in city parks and on the streets. Local advocates have been negotiating with the city to prevent the city from passing the law.

Measures that criminalize homelessness are legally problematic and do not make sense from a policy standpoint.

In Atlanta, Mayor Shirley Franklin issued an Executive Order prohibiting feeding homeless people in parks or in public. Although the order carries with it no legal sanction, it has deterred many churches and communities of faith from continuing with their food ministries.

Criminalization Violates Rights

Measures that criminalize homelessness are legally problematic and do not make sense from a policy standpoint. Laws that make it difficult for homeless persons to stay in downtown areas of cities force homeless persons away from crucial services and outreach. When a homeless person is arrested under one of these laws, he or she develops a criminal record, making it more difficult to obtain employment or housing. Further, criminalizing homelessness is an inefficient allocation of resources. It costs more to incarcerate someone than it does to provide supportive housing.

Homeless persons and advocates throughout the country have worked to prevent the passage of laws and to halt policies and practices that criminalize homelessness. Unfortunately, cities and police departments sometimes do not respond to such advocacy in any productive way. When local governments fail to respond to policy advocacy, homeless persons and their advocates have turned to litigation to end these laws and practices.

Courts have found begging to be protected speech.

As successful litigation has shown, many of the practices and policies that punish the public performance of life-sustaining activities by homeless persons violate the constitutional rights of homeless persons.

Rights to Panhandle and Sleep

One way that cities have targeted poor and homeless individuals is by passing laws that prohibit panhandling, solicitation, or begging. Depending on the scope of the ordinance, these types of laws can infringe on the right to free speech under the First Amendment. Courts have found begging to be protected speech. Laws that restrict speech too much, target speech based on its content, and do not allow for alternative channels of communication can violate the First Amendment.

Some courts have found laws that prohibit begging or panhandling unconstitutionally vague. A law is unconstitutionally vague if its language is not definite enough to give people notice of what is prohibited or if police could enforce the law in an arbitrary manner.

As many cities do not have adequate shelter space, homeless persons are often left with no alternative but to sleep and live in public spaces, such as sidewalks and parks. Even while cities are not dedicating enough resources to give homeless persons access to housing or shelters, some cities have enacted laws that impose criminal penalties upon people for sleeping outside. For example, in Atlanta, the law prohibits what is called "Urban Camping."

These punishments for sleeping outside have been challenged in courts for violating homeless persons' civil rights. Some courts have found that arresting homeless people for sleeping outside when no shelter space exists violates their Eighth Amendment right to be free from cruel and unusual punishment.

Advocates also have contended that arresting people for sleeping outside violates the fundamental right to travel. If people are arrested for sleeping in public in a city or certain areas of a city, those arrests have the effect of preventing homeless people from moving within a city or coming to a city, thereby interfering with their right to travel.

A Right to Be in Public Spaces

Another tool that cities have used to target people who live outside and on the streets are laws that prohibit loitering. Due to the broad scope of prohibited behavior under loitering laws, cities have used these to target homeless people in public spaces. Fortunately, cities have found these laws less useful, as the Supreme Court has overturned several loitering laws for being unconstitutionally vague.

In several cases, the Supreme Court has found vagrancy and loitering ordinances unconstitutional due to vagueness, in violation of the Due Process Clause of the Fourteenth Amendment of the Constitution. A statute is unconstitutionally vague if it does not give a person notice of prohibited conduct and encourages arbitrary police enforcement. Since many loitering laws have similarly broad and vague language, homeless persons and advocates have a strong argument that such laws violate the Due Process Clause of the Fourteenth Amendment.

Cities also target people experiencing homelessness by conducting sweeps of areas where a person or several persons are living outside. Sometimes, police or local government employees will go through an area where people are living and confiscate and destroy people's belongings in an attempt to "clean up" an area. While city workers may have the right to clean public areas, they must take certain measures to avoid violating people's right to be free from unreasonable searches and seizures guaranteed by the Fourth Amendment.

A seizure of property violates the Fourth Amendment when a governmental action unreasonably interferes with a person or his/her property. Courts have found that police practices of seizing and destroying personal property of homeless people violate these constitutional rights under the Fourth Amendment. In addition, some courts have also affirmed homeless persons' right to be free from unreasonable searches even if their belongings are stored in public spaces.

Litigation can protect the rights of homeless persons and pave the way for better city approaches to homelessness.

Some cities have passed laws that impose curfews on minors. These laws can pose problems for unaccompanied youth experiencing homelessness. Courts have overturned some of these laws for violating minors' right to free expression, right to freely move, and equal protection rights. In still other cities, many parks impose curfews.

Feeding as Religious Expression

Cities also have indirectly targeted homeless people by restricting service providers' feeding programs. Historically, cities have attempted to restrict feedings on providers' property through zoning laws. More recently, some cities have passed laws to restrict feedings in public spaces, such as parks. For faith-based or religious groups conducting feedings as an expression of their religious beliefs, courts have found city restrictions on feedings an unconstitutional burden on religious expression.

Litigation can protect the rights of homeless persons and pave the way for better city approaches to homelessness. Homeless persons bringing a civil action can receive damages or obtain injunctive or declaratory relief. In addition, many cases settle and result in policies or protocols that ensure homeless persons' rights will be protected.

Organizations to Contact

The editors have compiled the following list of organizations concerned with the issues debated in this book. The descriptions are derived from materials provided by the organizations. All have publications or information available for interested readers. The list was compiled on the date of publication of the present volume; names, addresses, and phone numbers may change. Be aware that many organizations take several weeks or longer to respond to inquiries, so allow as much time as possible.

American Enterprise Institute for Public Policy Research (AEI)
1150 Seventeenth Street NW, Washington, DC   20036
(202) 862-5800 • fax: (202) 862-7177
e-mail: webmaster@aei.org
Web site: www.aei.org

AEI is a private, nonpartisan, nonprofit institution dedicated to research and education on issues of government, politics, economics, and social welfare. It sponsors research and publishes materials with the aim of defending the principles, and improving the institutions, of American freedom and democratic capitalism. Among AEI's publications is the book *Prices, Poverty, and Inequality: Why Americans Are Better Off than You Think.*

Cato Institute
1000 Massachusetts Ave. NW, Washington, DC   20001-5403
(202) 842-0200 • fax: (202) 842-3490
Web site: www.cato.org

The Cato Institute is a public policy research foundation dedicated to limiting the role of government, protecting individual liberties, and promoting free markets. The institute commissions a variety of publications, including books, monographs, briefing papers, and other studies. Among its publications are the quarterly magazine *Regulation*, the bimonthly *Cato Policy Report*, and articles such as "More Welfare, More Poverty."

Center for Law and Social Policy (CLASP)

1015 Fifteenth Street NW, Suite 400, Washington, DC   20005
(202) 906-8000 • fax: (202) 842-2885
e-mail: info@clasp.org
Web site: www.clasp.org

The Center for Law and Social Policy is a national nonprofit that works to improve the lives of low-income people. It conducts research, provides policy analysis, advocates at the federal and state levels, and offers information and technical assistance on a range of family policy and equal justice issues. CLASP publishes many reports, briefs, and fact sheets, including the article "Sustaining Anti-Poverty Solutions: Keep an Eye on the Prize."

Center of Concern (COC)

1225 Otis Street NE, Washington, DC   20017
(202) 635-2757 • fax: (202) 832-9494
e-mail: coc@coc.org
Web site: www.coc.org

The Center of Concern is a faith-based organization working in collaboration with ecumenical and interfaith networks to bring a voice for social and economic justice to a global context. The COC challenges structural injustice and promotes innovative economic alternatives through analysis, education, advocacy, and capacity building. In addition to publishing the quarterly *Center Focus* newsletter, there are numerous publications available on its Web site, including the book *Opting for the Poor: The Challenge for the Twenty-first Century.*

Center on Budget and Policy Priorities

820 First Street NE, Suite 510, Washington, DC   20002
(202) 408-1080 • fax: (202) 408-1056

e-mail: center@cbpp.org
Web site: www.cbpp.org

The Center on Budget and Policy Priorities is a policy organization working at the federal and state levels on fiscal policy and public programs that affect low- and moderate-income families and individuals. The center conducts research and analysis to inform public debates over proposed budget and tax policies, and to help ensure that the needs of low-income families and individuals are considered in these debates. There are many reports available on its Web site, including "Food Stamp Benefits Falling Further Behind Rising Food Prices."

Children's Defense Fund (CDF)
25 E Street NW, Washington, DC   20001
(800) 233-1200
e-mail: cdfinfo@childrensdefense.org
Web site: www.childrensdefense.org

The Children's Defense Fund is a nonprofit child advocacy organization that works to ensure a level playing field for all American children, particularly poor and minority children and those with disabilities. The organization champions policies and programs that lift children out of poverty, including the Head Start and Healthy Start programs. The CDF publishes many reports, including "Improving Children's Health: Understanding Children's Health Disparities and Promising Approaches to Address Them," and "Katrina's Children: Still Waiting."

Coalition on Human Needs
1120 Connecticut Ave. NW, Suite 910
Washington, DC   20036
(202) 223-2532 • fax: (202) 223-2538
e-mail: info@chn.org
Web site: www.chn.org

The Coalition on Human Needs is an alliance of national organizations working together to promote public policies that address the needs of low-income and other vulnerable people.

The coalition promotes adequate funding for human needs programs, progressive tax policies, and other federal measures to address the needs of low-income and other vulnerable populations. The coalition publishes the *Human Needs Report* newsletter every other Friday when Congress is in session.

Economic Policy Institute (EPI)
1333 H Street NW, Suite 300, East Tower
Washington, DC   20005-4707
(202) 775-8810 • fax: (202) 775-0819
e-mail: researchdept@epi.org
Web site: www.epi.org

The Economic Policy Institute is a nonprofit, nonpartisan think tank that seeks to broaden the public debate about strategies to achieve a prosperous and fair economy. EPI conducts original research on economic issues, makes policy recommendations based on its findings, and disseminates its work to the appropriate audiences. Among the books, studies, issue briefs, popular education materials, and various other publications available are "The Economic Impact of Local Living Wages" and "What We Need to Get By."

National Alliance to End Homelessness
1518 K Street NW, Suite 410, Washington, DC   20005
(202) 638-1526 • fax: (202) 638-4664
e-mail: naeh@naeh.org
Web site: www.endhomelessness.org

The National Alliance to End Homelessness is a nonpartisan organization committed to preventing and ending homelessness in the United States. The organization develops policy solutions that help homeless individuals and families make positive changes in their lives, and provides research to policy makers and elected officials in order to inform policy debates. The organization provides fact sheets, reports, presentations, briefs, and case studies on its Web site, including "The 2007 Annual Homeless Assessment Report: A Summary of Findings."

National Coalition for Homeless Veterans (NCHV)
333½ Pennsylvania Ave. SE
Washington, DC   20003-1148
(800) VET-HELP • fax: (888) 233-8582
e-mail: nchv2@nchv.org
Web site: www.nchv.org

The National Coalition for Homeless Veterans is a nonprofit organization that operates as a resource and technical assistance center for a national network of agencies that provide emergency and supportive housing, food, health services, job training and placement assistance, legal aid, and case management support for hundreds of thousands of homeless veterans each year. NCHV works to end homelessness among veterans by shaping public policy, promoting collaboration, and building the capacity of service providers. NCHV publishes information to provide assistance to community and faith-based organizations, government agencies, corporate partners, and the homeless veterans they serve.

National Coalition for the Homeless (NCH)
2201 P Street NW, Washington, DC   20037
(202) 462-4822 • fax: (202) 462-4823
e-mail: info@nationalhomeless.org
Web site: www.nationalhomeless.org

The National Coalition For the Homeless is a national network of people who are currently experiencing or who have experienced homelessness, activists and advocates, community-based and faith-based service providers, and others committed to ending homelessness. The NCH works to meet the immediate needs of people who are currently experiencing homelessness or who are at risk of doing so. Among the NCH reports and papers available at its Web site is "Hate, Violence, and Death on Main Street USA: A Report on Hate Crimes and Violence Against People Experiencing Homelessness."

Bibliography

Books

Cynthia J. Bogard *Seasons Such as These: How Homelessness Took Shape in America.* New York: Aldine de Gruyter, 2003.

Kurt Borchard *The Word on the Street: Homeless Men in Las Vegas.* Reno: University of Nevada Press, 2005.

Rachel G. Bratt, Michael E. Stone, and Chester Hartman, eds. *A Right to Housing: Foundation for a New Social Agenda.* Philadelphia: Temple University Press, 2006.

Jason DeParle *American Dream: Three Women, Ten Kids, and a Nation's Drive to End Welfare.* New York: Penguin, 2005.

Leonard C. Feldman *Citizens Without Shelter: Homelessness, Democracy, and Political Exclusion.* Ithaca, NY: Cornell University Press, 2004.

Marni Finkelstein *With No Direction Home: Homeless Youth on the Road and in the Streets.* Belmont, CA: Thomson/Wadsworth, 2005.

Sharon Hays *Flat Broke with Children: Women in the Age of Welfare Reform.* New York: Oxford University Press, 2004.

John Iceland   *Poverty in America: A Handbook.*
                      Berkeley and Los Angeles: University
                      of California Press, 2006.

Jeff Karabanow   *Being Young and Homeless:*
                      Understanding How Youth Enter and
                      Exit Street Life. New York: Peter
                      Lang, 2004.

Charles H. Karelis   *The Persistence of Poverty: Why the*
                      Economics of the Well-Off Can't Help
                      the Poor. New Haven, CT: Yale
                      University Press, 2007.

Anthony Marcus   *Where Have All the Homeless Gone?*
                      The Making and Unmaking of a
                      Crisis. New York: Berghahn Books,
                      2006.

Paul Milbourne   *International Perspective on Rural*
and Paul Cloke,   *Homelessness.* New York: Routledge,
eds.   2006.

Stephen Pimpare   *A People's History of Poverty in*
                      America. New York: New Press, 2008.

Mark Robert   *One Nation, Underprivileged: Why*
Rank   *American Poverty Affects Us All.* New
                      York: Oxford University Press, 2005.

Paul A. Rollinson   *Homelessness in Rural America: Policy*
and John T.   *and Practice.* New York: Haworth,
Pardeck   2006.

Jeffrey Sachs   *The End of Poverty: Economic*
                      Possibilities for Our Time. New York:
                      Penguin, 2006.

David K. Shipler   *The Working Poor: Invisible in America*. New York: Vintage Books, 2005.

Michael D. Tanner   *The Poverty of Welfare: Helping Others in Civil Society*. Washington, DC: Cato Institute, 2003.

Periodicals

America   "Homelessness: A Solvable Problem," March 5, 2007.

Emily Amick   "Marrying Absurd: The Bush Administration's Attempts to Encourage Marriage," *Nation*, March 6, 2007. www.thenation.com.

Laverne Ballard   "God Bless the Child: A Woman Who Grew Up Sleeping in the Streets Tells Her Haunting Story," *Essence*, September 2006.

Dean Barnett   "The Last Talking Point of the Left," *Weekly Standard*, November 19, 2007.

Alyssa Katharine Ritz Battistoni   "The Reality of Poverty," *Nation*, October 8, 2007. www.thenation.com.

Peter D. Bell   "We Have the Tools to End Global Poverty: Empowering Individuals by Meeting Basic Needs Is a Start," *Christian Science Monitor*, March 22, 2006.

Nate Berg   "Who's Poor? It Depends on Where You Live, Some Say," *Christian Science Monitor*, August 26, 2008.

David Callahan	"False Choices on Poverty," *American Prospect*, April 22, 2007.
Christian Science Monitor	"Headway with the Homeless," August 28, 2008.
Greg J. Duncan	"High-Quality Preschool as Antipoverty," *American Prospect*, May 2007.
Economic Opportunity Report	"Criminalization of Homelessness Is on the Rise in Cities Nationwide," January 23, 2006.
Kevin Fagan	"S.F. Man Is Homeless—by Choice," *San Francisco Chronicle*, January 2, 2004.
Les Gapay	"How a Regular Guy Gets Homeless," *USA Today*, September 22, 2003.
Bob Herbert	"American Cities and the Great Divide," *New York Times*, May 22, 2007.
Bruce Hetrick	"2006 Years Later and Still No Room at the Inn," *Indianapolis Business Journal*, December 18, 2006.
Phillip Hozer	"'Get a Job!' Eight Myths and Misconceptions About People Who Are Homeless," *Cross Currents: The Journal of Addiction and Mental Health*, Summer 2006.
Nicholas D. Kristof	"The Larger Shame," *New York Times*, September 6, 2005.

Paul Krugman   "Helping the Poor, the British Way," *New York Times*, December 25, 2006.

Robert Kuttner   "Compassion and Coalition," *American Prospect*, May 2007.

Mark Lange   "A First Step for the Global Poor—Shatter Six Myths," *Christian Science Monitor*, March 10, 2008.

Carrissa Larsen   "Homeless by Choice—the New Trend," *Associated Content*, November 3, 2006.

Barry Loberfeld   "What About the Poor?" *FrontPage Magazine*, August 13, 2008. www.frontpagemag.com.

Steven Malanga   "The Myth of the Working Poor," *City Journal*, November 30, 2004.

Maurice Martin   "Living Wage Offers Ray of Light for Homeless," *People's Weekly World*, May 19, 2005.

Douglas W. Nelson   "Counting What Counts: A Better Way to Define Poverty," *Washington Times*, August 29, 2007.

New York Times   "Counting the Poor," April 17, 2007.

Eyal Press   "The New Suburban Poverty," *Nation*, April 13, 2007.

Robert E. Rector   "How Poor Are America's Poor? Examining the 'Plague' of Poverty in America," Heritage Foundation, August 27, 2007. www.heritage.org.

Alan Reynolds   "Poverty Puffery," *Washington Times*, September 11, 2005.

Bill Steigerwald   "Are Our 37 Million Poor Really Poor?" *Townhall.com*, September 11, 2007. www.townhall.com.

Syracuse (NY)   "Ending Homelessness: Nation's
Post-Standard   'Homelessness Czar' Pushes a New Prescription to Cure a Costly Social Ill," September 30, 2007.

Michael Tanner   "More Welfare, More Poverty," *Charlotte (NC) Observer*, September 12, 2006.

Liz Welch   "No Place Called Home: Homelessness in the United States Is on the Rise—and Many of the People Forced Out of Their Homes Are Under 25. Why Is This Happening?" *CosmoGirl!* May 2004.

Brian S. Williams   "We All Pay the Price of Homelessness," *Indianapolis Business Journal*, September 19, 2005.

Scott Winship   "Welfare Reform Worked—Don't Fix
and Christopher   It," *Christian Science Monitor*, July 21,
Jencks   2004.

Index